PET, PET, SLAP

Andrew Battershill

Coach House Books, Toronto

first edition

Published with the generous assistance of the Canada Council for the Arts and the Ontario Arts Council. Coach House Books also acknowledges the support of the Government of Canada through the Canada Book Fund and the Government of Ontario through the Ontario Book Publishing Tax Credit.

LIBRARY AND ARCHIVES CANADA CATALOGUING IN PUBLICATION

Title: Pet, pet, slap / Andrew Battershill.
Names: Battershill, Andrew, 1988- author.
Identifiers: Canadiana (print) 20240289765 | Canadiana (ebook) 20240289781 | ISBN 9781552454763 (softcover) | ISBN 9781770568006 (PDF) | ISBN 9781770567993 (EPUB)
Subjects: LCGFT: Novels.
Classification: LCC PS8603.A876 P48 2024 | DDC C813/.6—dc23

Pet, Pet, Slap is available as an ebook: ISBN 978 1 77056 799 3 (EPUB), ISBN 978 1 77056 800 6 (PDF)

Purchase of the print version of this book entitles you to a free digital copy. To claim your ebook of this title, please email sales@chbooks.com with proof of purchase. (Coach House Books reserves the right to terminate the free digital download offer at any time.)

I'm not worried. I know what I have to do. I'm going to go out here and dazzle myself. I'm going to surprise myself with how good I'm going to look.

– Pernell Whitaker

Part 1

Pillow Slips

I.

If you're lying flat on your back snuggling your sloth best friend, the sloth will have this natural reaction of grasping his weird domed hands around the back of your head and sliding his face across your chin. Pillow had asked the exotic animal dealer why, and it's because a sloth is stupid enough to keep hoping you're a tree, even if he knows you're not. Even as he listens to your heartbeat, a sloth is stupid and beautiful and hopeful enough to keep rubbing that chin in case it turns into a branch and a pear falls off.

Pillow kissed the abrasive hair on his sloth's face. 'What can I do, Jersey Joe?' The sloth stopped for a very long minute, as sloths do, and then pressed his head back down. 'I'm sorry, Jersey Joe. I'm gonna miss you so bad, and I'm so sorry.'

Pillow was in the middle of fucking up very badly. That was a thing he knew. The thing he didn't know was what exact thing he was fucking up. Any time you're eight weeks out from a professional fist fight and you're gakked out on pharmaceutical-grade cocaine kissing a sloth on a couch worth more than your stock portfolio, your training camp is not going great. So, sure, he was fucking up his training camp; that was obvious, but if he was fucking up his training camp, was he also fucking up his boxing career? And if you're fucking up your boxing career, you're fucking up your whole life. You're making yourself forget things that haven't even happened yet. You're embarrassing yourself in a nursing home that hasn't been built yet in front of a sweet, sad nurse who hasn't been born yet. You're slurring words you haven't said yet, and you're already slurring that dull insistence that you didn't just slur all the words you slurred.

The boxer moved his face to the back of his sloth's neck and kissed the spot the sloth liked to be scratched. A kiss is different from a scratch in some very specific way important to sloths. Pillow scratched and Jersey Joe yawned his giant circular head pleasurably toward the hand. 'Do you ever dream about being air? Just evaporating and then sitting in a room with everyone you love and just getting breathed in and out. Whoever's there, whoever comes, they can just breathe you in and out and then leave and breathe someone else.' For a while there was just silence and the sound a mansion makes when there are just three people and a sloth in it. 'I guess that was me telling you a secret, Jersey Joe, because I do. I dream that when I'm feeling good.'

There are a lot of ways you end up eight weeks out from the last of your last shots against an Olympic gold medallist four inches taller and twenty pounds heavier than you, out of shape, kissing your sloth best friend goodbye and starting to cry now, and which way you picked doesn't matter much. However you did it, you end up knowing you're saying goodbye because every day your sloth best friend spent with you was torture for him. Even as he hugs your face, you know it's only because he's too stupid to ever understand what you are, let alone how you are.

Pillow loved animals. The weirder the better. And because he was a person who just one day, without even really meaning to, had enough money to fly to a private zoo in Tennessee and buy a sloth and then fly to a mansion in Miami and buy a shark and bring both animals home to his giant empty house, Pillow had been able to spend every day with nature's sharpest, meanest, weirdest and its meekest, slowest, and weirdest. And all it had done was remind Pillow that dreams can't come true. Either dreams are real right when you have them or they're not.

Jean Painlevé peeked his head around the door. 'Pillow, they can't wait any longer.'

Because he knew Jersey Joe didn't have the emotional capacity to be offended by it, Pillow yanked him by the fur collar so he could look, one more time, into the sloth's perfectly round, perfectly empty eyes. He just looked, which is mostly what you end up doing with animals. 'I'll miss you, Joe. I love you so much.'

Painlevé grabbed Jersey Joe under the sloth's long, creepy arms and pulled him off, and Jersey Joe hooked those arms around Jean's face and nuzzled him, hoping this man was a tree and that this tree had fruit. 'You're doing the right thing, Pillow. He'll be happier.'

Pillow sat up and looked at the criss-crossing surgical scars across the top of his right hand, then he used the hand to rub his fat, flat nose. In four hours, he was supposed to run five miles and then he was supposed to drink a smoothie and do 1,000 sit-ups. He closed one eye, because it felt like the right thing to do. 'Yeah. That's what we'll all be someday.'

2.

Pillow still loved boxing. It was just that over the years, he'd come to hate work. At the start, work had been the whole world and Pillow had loved the whole world. Running without headphones, just his breath in his ears, feet on the ground, thinking boxing the whole time. Always boxing. Always work. Then, he got paid. And this beautiful thing he did wasn't work anymore, it was a job. Once you're at a job, it's not about devoting yourself to it, it's about exploiting the guy paying you more than he exploits you. Getting a little out of a lot. That morning, he'd done two of his five miles, enough to get a sweat on, enough to sell it to Kim.

Kim Lion was Pillow's trainer. They were an unlikely pairing, a quirky mismatch. Kim had been one of the best female boxers of all time, and her style had been the exact opposite of Pillow's. Pillow was 'Pillow Fist' Pete Wilson, the lightest-hitting boxer in the world. Smooth, slick, defensive, couldn't punch a lick and didn't really want to. All style, no substance. Kim had been a seek-and-destroy knockout puncher. Physically, she looked a lot like a truck whose motor ate glass instead of burning gas. Socially, she vibed a lot like a truck who ate glass and snacked on tar sand. But she and Pillow worked well together. After Pillow lost his title, he'd fired his coaches and gone for a workout with Kim, recently retired and looking to train fighters. Pillow went to her gym mostly out of curiosity, to maybe get a fresh look and some new sparring partners. Kim had been a crude fighter, more physically gifted than smart or technical, and nobody was taking her all that seriously as a coach. One training session was all it took. They'd been together ever since.

In their hearts, boxers love negativity. They want to see someone get beat ten times more than they want to see someone win.

And for that reason, fighters have the most respect for the styles opposite to their own. Brawlers love boxers, and boxers love knockout artists. When Pillow watched defensive boxers, he was always tearing them down, nitpicking the details. When he watched brawlers, he saw all the cute tricks they used to break people down. All the subtleties they didn't get credit for. Kim had spent her boxing life walking down cute slicksters like Pillow and faceplanting them, but when she watched a fight, she rooted for the fighter on the back foot.

While she'd always love him as a boxer, Pillow had a feeling this was the last camp she'd put up with him as a person. Even having done less than half the run he was supposed to, Pillow had needed to pick up some greenies before training if he was going to make it through the day, so he was twenty minutes late walking through the door of Kim's gym, the Lion's Den.

Kim didn't look away from the two teenage amateurs pawing at each other, but her voice boomed out like gunshot making love to a giant metal cup. 'Motherfucker, this is my last camp with you. For real.'

Pillow grinned. He swished some water around his dry mouth and spit it into the floor drain. He geared up slowly in the open space of the gym, stopping to give about twenty fist bumps to random lower-level fighters.

Kim was obviously pissed, so he grabbed a welterweight to help him run through his warm-up. After he was loose and lathered, Pillow shuffled up behind Kim and set to shadowboxing about a foot away from her until she paid attention to him. She shot half of one eye in his direction.

'Am I supposed to be impressed that you're sweating?'

Pillow reeled off sixteen upcuts, cut an angle, and jabbed out. 'If you're in awe, are you impressed?'

Kim did her best to snort, which didn't work great since she had about a quarter of a nostril's breath through her nose these days. 'No.' She fired a snot rocket at the ground, rubbed it out with the toe of her shoe. 'Let's start with ten 100s on the heavy bag.'

'C'mon, let's just spar.'

'I know you can half-ass-carry your way through rounds with sparring partners. Can you go full blast on the fuckin' cardio-box program with the business ladies at lunchtime? That's what we're only guessing.'

'I'll fight this kid tomorrow. I'm in shape.'

'You know that a piece of shit is in a shape, right? Something exists, it's in a shape.'

'That's what you said last time.'

'Last time you fought a club fighter on a month's notice. This time you're fighting the Golden Boy.'

Pillow fired a one-two and rolled under an imaginary left hook. 'You can say I'm not working hard, but you can give me anyone to spar. I'm fighting a man, not a bagful of sand.' He double jabbed then pulled an imaginary right hand and sunk an imaginary uppercut into an imaginary gut. Kim sighed and reached out to smack his forehead, and Pillow seamlessly rolled it, circled out, and hit his imaginary friend with a walk-off check hook, then bounced into skipping an imaginary rope.

Kim wagged a finger at him. 'I will stop this fight before the bell rings for Round One if you not in the shape you need to be in. Work now.'

Pillow stopped moving and sized her up. Then he did an hour of hard work with Kim, went six rounds of life-or-death sparring with a mediocre junior welterweight, vomited bile in the bathroom, and shuffled back out to cool off and stretch.

In the last few years, Pillow had relaxed on all the rules he'd been given as a kid and on all the things he'd known. He'd been a young hotshot, got his first step-up fight at twenty-two, and clearly, bravely, lost on points to a bigger, older, better fighter. A year later, Pillow had his first comeback, which had lasted six fights and three years. He'd won his title and defended it three times against game but overmatched mandatory challengers. It had all come easier, and for the first time ever, he'd had fun. His first shot at the big time had been joy and fulfilment and feeling like the tiny hole where his actual self was wasn't a hole at all but a hulking mountain of work and winning and always knowing what to do. The second run had been fun. It had been going to the zoo and making friends and fucking. Going to the club, and then sweating it all out in the morning, finishing at the gym with his whole body clean, cleared out, and putting on a smooth, clean, perfect silk shirt with 200 pictures of the same smooth, clean, perfect hammerhead shark on it and going home and looking at the shark that was his living room wall. Living his life at maximum voltage and being slick enough to get away with it.

And for his second big-money fight against an elite fighter, his third once-in-a-lifetime opportunity, Pillow had shit the bed. Thrown zero punches, had no juice, run out of ideas, and gotten stopped in ten rounds. It was after that he'd hooked up with Kim, who'd seen him through his second comeback, and now she'd be here for the third and almost certainly for-real-last shot at the big time.

Now, he was fighting Julio Solis, a soon-to-be superstar, for the short money and a shot at the belt. And, for the first time in a long while, because Jean Painlevé the nature documentarian had explained animal ethics to him, he'd have to do it without his pets.

Kim sat beside him on the bench and rubbed his head. 'Good work, bubba. Today was all right. But you see what I'm saying?'

'Yeah, I need to get in shape.'

'Can't be suckin' wind after six rounds with a 140-pounder. You know it.'

Pillow grabbed her head and kissed the top of her braids. 'We know it.'

Kim laughed and punched her blunt fist into her thick, cracked palm. 'I know you're older and you know your body. I respect you, Pedro, I do, baby, but this camp, just this camp, let's go easy. You stay home, you watch movies. Do some yoga. No partying, nothing. You barely got time to even get in shape.'

'Kid's got nothing. Hype job. Easy work.'

Kim shook her head. 'So, make him easy. Just give me seven weeks hard training. Deal?'

'Deal.'

They shook on it and Kim went back to the ring. Pillow looked at his hands, which were shaking harder than most people would say was good. His whole body was doing a whole lot more of a whole lot of things than most people would say was any good at all.

3.

As a successful boxer, Pillow faced a constant stream of requests from community charities and youth groups. Because he was a sketchy man who smoked weed and thought about his life sometimes, once every few months, shame would wash over him and he'd say yes. Most of the time, he just sent money, but sometimes he didn't have much on hand, and other times he'd think about how sad it is to just throw money at people with otherwise shitty lives, and he'd convince himself that this time it'd be fine, he could do a youth camp.

He'd show up and either the coaches would be weird and craven or, more often, they'd be sweet, slightly formal middle-aged men who'd be super nice the whole time and then make everyone join a group prayer at the end. However hard he tried to remind himself of their decency, Pillow couldn't help but have his teeth set on edge by these people. Always, no matter how nice or accommodating they were, they wanted Pillow to be something he couldn't: an example of the way the world could eventually be good for poor children.

Pillow would coach the kids, have some fun, and then get prodded into saying something inspiring. All the kids looking at him, Pillow would take an awkward pause, crack a joke, and tell a story. The god-fearing coach would wrinkle his brow and rephrase it to the kids, taking the exact opposite meaning than Pillow'd intended, somehow hearing a story about going into a fight with a broken hand and winning because your opponent broke his foot and telling the kids it was about fate and courage.

Pillow sensed the clump of kids, the church-deacon energy of the coach from a distance. Turning the corner into the gym, he waved apologetically. 'Sorry I'm late.'

The coach was more of a shape than a guy Pillow was looking at. 'No apologies, no apologies needed, brother. It's great for these kids to see … We are so grateful to have you here. Kids, let's stand and clap for this man.'

For the few seconds it needed to, Pillow's consciousness left his body. Pillow's consciousness was good that way.

When he was twelve years old, Pillow had been assigned as a Big Brother a sweaty square with three round bubbles on the front named Daryl, who owned apartment buildings and was on probation for corporate fraud. After their third meeting, as Pillow wolfed a Whopper and a milkshake, Daryl told him that he seemed like a sharp kid who knew how things worked, and he'd asked Pillow what he wanted in exchange for signing the attendance slips. Pillow thought it over and told Daryl that six months of fees at the boxing gym around the corner from his house and a hundred-dollar gift card for the movie theatre would do the trick. Daryl had frowned and chewed a fry and told him to forget the gift card. Pillow slurped some milkshake and asked Daryl how much money 120 hours was worth to a Big Brother. Daryl reached out a day-old charcuterie plate that was also his hand and made the deal.

It was another of the stories Pillow told that people took exactly the wrong way. Most people would shake their heads and say the Correct Opinion as if it was a thought they'd had. Even chill people would laugh and say *what a piece of shit*. To Pillow, Daryl was the best Big Brother in history. He'd seemed awesome at the time, and life unfolding had only proven him better. Most of the other kids got boring Jesus-y types who would take them to a pond, sit ramrod straight on a bench, and tell them about how important school and effort and humility are. How one day, if you just try hard enough and thank everybody every minute of your life, you too might have a mediocre pension and an expensive couch on which to watch television until you die. Daryl had met Pillow, sized him up accurately, and given everyone a good deal.

Other kids had gotten twenty-five awkward afternoons with guys they'd never hang out with by choice. Pillow had gotten a livelihood, a craft, eight R-rated movies, and five giant popcorns.

After a quick introduction, during which he accidentally made it extremely clear he had not forgotten the coach's name but rather that the coach's name had never for one second touched any corner of his mind, Pillow got the kids started with a footwork drill that doubled as a warm-up. Their feet were all over the place. It was obviously a get-the-kids-off-the-street gym rather than a competitive one. That was fine. Pillow liked it when the kids were there for fun, but he'd never tried to figure out a beginner's workout. He just ran the same drills he always did.

After being held back from sixth grade for emotional problems, Pillow had briefly been the fastest 1,600-metre runner at his school before getting kicked off the track team for fighting a kid whose runners he'd stolen at Regionals. He'd really kicked the shit out of the kid. After that, Pillow felt pretty sure he could fight, and that even though he was terrible at ball sports, he had what it took to be a boxer. There was even a gym around the corner from his house. Daryl showed up at the perfect time, cash in hand.

Daryl had driven Pillow to the gym, paid his dues, and not seen him again until the farewell evaluation with the PO, which they'd passed by saying there had been long conversations about careers and trips to the driving range. Daryl had given him a clammy hundred-dollar bill and a fist bump, cementing his status as a Good Fucking Guy. Pillow had still never held a golf club.

At these youth gigs there's a lot of bullshit about how everybody sucks at the beginning. They say it because most people suck at most things, and if you're running a camp you have to say something. The reality is that most people who are good at something were good at it immediately. It takes work and you learn, but if something's ever going to be there, talentwise, there'll be some kind of glimmer at the very start.

After his first class at the gym, a sketchy guy with a milky right eye had pulled Pillow aside and asked him what gym he'd come from. When Pillow told him it was his first class, the guy had run a hand through his greasy hair and whistled and led him straight to Boots.

Boots Frutch was not a famous trainer. He looked, sounded, acted, and coached exactly like people everybody calls the 'the best trainers in the game,' but nobody outside the local amateur circuit knew who he was. Boots looked anywhere from a rough fifty to a well-preserved eighty years old. A rail-thin guy with a salt-and-pepper flat-top, always wearing a giant bowling shirt and loose, faded-almost-to-white blue jeans. Boots had been a semi-promising prospect, his career cut short when he'd shot his own big toe off during a jewellery store robbery and caught four years.

Pillow had watched the one-eyed floor-mopper whisper in Boots's ear for a bit. Boots looked him up and down, chewed an ancient piece of gum for a while, and motioned Pillow over. He had this quiet, high voice, like it came straight from his lungs through a balloon and ended up in your ear.

'What's your name?'

'Pete.'

'Travis says you can move a bit. That was really your first class?'

'Yeah.'

'You're not lying?'

'No.'

'You play sports?'

'I ran 1,600 metres. I was the best in my school. Third place in counties.'

'You say ran. Why don't you run anymore, you're so good?'

'I got kicked off for fighting.'

'For fighting?'

'For winning a fight, yeah.'

A grin slowly folded Boot's cheek in three sections. He looked up at Travis. 'For winning a fight, he says.' They laughed, and Pillow was instantly enraged in a familiar way. Adults acting like you weren't even in the room. Like you were drapes if drapes could also be actively stupid. This time, though, he held his tongue, sensing something good coming. 'All right, Pete, how about you show me what you saw in class just now? What you remember.'

Whatever he'd showed had been good enough. Those first six months of fees a greasy slumlord had paid for him were the last gym fees Pillow would ever pay. Boots floated him, used gym money to pay his tournament entries until he turned pro. They'd built him up the way they did any prospect, finding him a style. Putting him in against older, bigger fighters to beat him down in the gym, see if he could take it, then letting him loose at the tournaments. He didn't win every time, but he won a lot. Boots always there, always with something new to add. Thinking back on it, Pillow knew that was the best thing Boots did with him, never talking about what they were going to fix, only what they were going to add. That tiny hollow voice: 'another thing for you to think about, here.' Then, a new step, a new angle, some new feint. And Pillow learned it all. He was the most naturally talented kid at the gym, and he was the most dedicated student.

After seeing that his drills were way above the kids' level, Pillow let the coach run the class and ambled around correcting form. He asked the kids if they were having a good time, and they all said yes. It might even have been a bit fun for him if he didn't know the speech was coming. The questions. What inspired him?

Most youth coaches were Big Brother types, thinking you could teach lessons about being a Good Man through punching. Pillow knew that when you teach someone how to punch better, all they learn is how to be a better puncher. Most of these coaches were tell-you-a-life-lesson-and-listen-long-enough-to-hear-you-say-it-back guys. And his whole life, that had never been who'd helped him.

Boots wasn't some father figure. He never gave you life advice, he just said what you had to do. He never trained pros, he never travelled. He just showed up at the gym every single day, took his tiny salary, and went home to his tiny apartment. He wasn't some tragic, overlooked genius. He was a simple guy who could only ever make sense of one thing: teaching kids the very beginning of perfect boxing. You couldn't show Boots tape of your opponent and have him come up with a game plan. You couldn't ask him about promoters or management or taking the right fights. He knew the basics, and he understood the beauty of those basics in a small, profound way. But that was all.

After the class, they all sat down. The kids all in a semicircle sweaty and smiling. Partially to kill time and partially to be nice, Pillow moved around the circle and gave everyone a high-five. Then, he tried to take as long as possible telling them that the important thing was to be physically active and have fun with your friends. He hadn't planned it in advance, and he knew from experience that he couldn't be trusted to keep it PG off-the-cuff, so he winced and turned it over to questions.

Zero hesitation, Deacon Energy thanked him another twelve times, then said: 'Since you've been inspiring us, I have to turn it back around. What inspires you?'

Pillow didn't so much think about the question as he thought about thinking about it. 'Uh, good question. Um. I'd say that, uh, fun. I love to have fun. There's a difference between fu– messing around and really having fun. Putting in some thought and enjoying yourself. So, that's what I'm trying to do. I'm trying to have a good time, mostly.'

Deacon Energy nodded slowly, as if tasting what Pillow was saying. 'So, you're talking about joy. You're saying joy inspires you.'

And hearing it said back, that actually was what Pillow meant. 'Yes.'

'Wonderful, wonderful. Inspiring words, my brother, inspiring words. Let's turn it over to the kids.'

Pillow told them to ask any questions they wanted. Most of the questions were about his fights, and he gave them the funniest G-rated answers he could. Finally, a chubby kid in the back raised his hand and asked how to know if you're going to make it as a boxer.

Pillow looked at the kid and grimaced a little. 'You say you, you mean me, right? Like how do *I*,' he pointed at the kid, 'know if I'm going to make it as a professional? Not a hobby, not fighting amateurs, the real shit … the real thing, sorry.'

The kid set his mouth and nodded. 'Yeah. How can we know if we can be pro?'

Pillow believed strongly that the least you owe a kid is the truth. 'The day you turn pro you also turn into a huckleberry. That's a fact. Every-single-body's huckleberry, that's me. For advice, I'd say you should train hard, enter some tournaments, and see how you do. Win a few of those, you ask yourself *Am I the best guy at my gym?* And be really, really honest. Are you kicking everybody's ass in sparring? If yes, go try to get a legit trainer. Train hard for a year, ask yourself again, then ask him. Keep asking, and if either one of you ever says no, quit right that second. For real. Maybe you'll get better, but the guys better than you will get better too. Maybe as a long shot you'd have caught up eventually. But that's a long shot, and when you're gambling with ass-kickings you should only ever bet chalk. It's boxing. There's no podium and there there's no finish line. You're the best or you're fucked up, bleeding on a stool. That's it.'

Pillow had sort of spaced out staring at the wall above the kids as he was talking. He came back to himself and saw what twelve twelve-year-olds and a deeply kind, deeply dull probably Deacon look like when they're absolutely horrified

4.

That evening, Pillow skipped his mobility session to shoot liquid cocaine with his roommate, Sherlock Holmes. Holmes was explaining just how sad and small a thing it is to deduce something.

After his last big fight, Pillow had put the $200K he had left after taxes on the street with Gwynn Apollinaire, a local gang leader and generally awesome lady, and had gotten back $300K and half a key for personal use. Flush with more cash and blow than he knew what to do with, Pillow had followed Gwynn's advice and reinvested the cash into a private chemistry lab in his basement for Sherlock.

Sherlock had been balling out in London as this world-class PI before he burned out on the game (and his massive coke habit), and straight up faked falling off a waterfall to get out. The great detective wandered the earth for a bit, then hunkered down in Pillow's basement to brew better pharmaceutical-grade coke, uppers, Xanax, and Soviet mystery potions than you could find anywhere on the street. Or the sidewalk. Or the highway. Or on the tracks of a train that goes faster than a fighter jet just from using magnets.

'You see, dear Pillow, the impulse to deduce is the polar opposite of the creative urge. To be a detective is to be forever eliminating, forever paring down. Forever saying no. You observe things, and you note them in the event that some future thing will strike a discordant note with them. That you'll be able to say another no to the world. All that time, never making a thing. Eventually one must ask if anything is ever made.'

Pillow's heart was beating incredibly quickly in a perfect rhythm. He stood up and started shadowboxing. 'You're making all the shit now, baby, WOO!'

Holmes was a not-halfway-bad amateur boxer, and he gangled his way, a foot of limb at a time, to his feet and started shadow sparring. Matching Pillow's feints and steps at about half the speed. They moved around as they talked, Pillow's toes beating Sherlock's to every spot.

'See, Pillow, the truth of the matter is that nothing is created in a chemical undertaking. Things that are find themselves bluntly combined into what already could have been. Those elements may be combined with more or less expertise or in a manner that embodies or lacks a creative impulse, but nothing has been made, by the very laws of this random universe.'

Pillow missed his sloth. He L-stepped out, settled, and, seeing the spot for it, imagined his fist slamming into the hinge of Sherlock's jaw.

The detective grinned and stiffly slipped to his right hip, arm extended out in front of him like he was fighting bare-knuckle in dropped-down overalls. He bowed and hit a tight ballet spin as he approached his violin stand. Pillow didn't know what song he started playing right then, but it felt like it started suddenly and in the middle, and now the world was swimming-pool-full of classical music he'd fallen in.

The music kept up and Pillow's imagination took over. He picked up the pace and ended up shadowboxing for real, seeing his opponent, Julio Solis: the guy's moves, his capped delts, the way he tracked the centreline with his left hand, pulled it back just a little slow after his jab. Sherlock played all of something long, and Pillow worked through it, no rounds, and by the time they both stopped and sat back down on the couch, he'd soaked his clothes through.

Sherlock grabbed his deepest pipe and did that cool huffing-puffing thing to start it, waiting for Pillow to get his wind back. 'You look quite good for someone who looks like shit.'

Pillow laughed. 'That's the best I look these days. Best for either of us.'

Sherlock smiled. 'Different species of excrement, but you know the saying: dog shit looks more like cat shit than it looks like a dog.'

'That is so true.'

Aside from introducing him to the concept of passive income, the main benefit of Pillow's Sherlock lab investment was that Pillow now had a straight, no middle-man-snitches pipeline to the performance-enhancing drugs he needed, the performance-crushing drugs he wanted, and the tricks to beat any test for both. Sherlock had turned out to be an unrivalled doping whiz.

Sherlock went to his desk, retrieved the vial Pillow had initially come for, and tossed it over. 'That should see you through the week.'

Pillow's heart was beating very, very quickly, and he thought, for just a second, about how many more times his heart had beat than most people his age. 'I'm in a bad way, Sherlock.'

'I had deduced such.' Sherlock's hands shook as he needlessly started his pipe again.

'I'm gonna beat this kid's ass, though.'

'Of course.'

'Motherfucker couldn't catch me with a net. I just have to get my wind right. So, thanks for this.' The vial wiggled between Pillow's fingers. 'Say Sherlock, I've been thinking about something, wanted to run it by you.'

Sherlock waved him on, then blew three perfect smoke rings.

'I was doing my run this morning. And I was thinking about that saying: the early bird gets the worm, right?'

Sherlock nodded. 'That rarest of folk wisdom with which I agree, and that most common piece of folk wisdom which I fail, each day, to heed.'

'I wake up at five in the morning my whole life because the early bird gets the worm. But I've been giving away my pets, right? So, I'm thinking about trying to think about what animals need.

What they really need and think about and want, and I think now, what about the early worm? What does he get?'

Two long smoke rings drifted into the nothing of air.

'The early worm, he gets fucked in the face, is what he gets.' Pillow sucked his teeth, his tongue lingering, as it always did, on the cheap little piece of gold where he used to have a tiny expensive bone. 'So, we say that assuming we're all birds. And we both know, Sherlock, most people most of the time are worms. And if you're a worm, you better remember it when you're setting the alarm clock, you feel me?'

Sherlock's pipe was somehow out again and he sucked on it dry three times before trembling it back to the coffee table. He leaned back into the couch and ran his hands through the full path of his widow's peak, his toe still tapping out the rhythm of a sonata. 'I am loathe to admit that at this exact moment I am not in the business of feeling terribly many things.'

'Speaking of which, let's cool this off with some opium so I can get to sleep.'

'That … ' Sherlock got back to standing in three distinct stages, stretching his brutally locked up back at the top, 'is elementary, dear Pillow.'

5.

Kim wrapped Pillow's hands as he watched his sparring partner shifting his weight from one leg to the other in the corner. The kid was hyped up, ready to go. Pillow smiled to himself and watched as Kim layered on the gauze past all legal limits to protect his right hand.

Pillow skipped forward as his opponent walked to centre ring and they touched gloves. As was his way, Pillow took it easy in the first two rounds, controlling the distance and smothering on the rare occasions he got cut off. Right before Kim called time on Round Two, the kid faked a jab to the stomach, and Pillow reached to parry and took a hard, leaping left hook to the side of the head.

Kim hit Pillow in the face with a wet sponge as he got to the corner, the water dripping off his headgear.

'You feeling cute?'

Pillow spit his mouthguard into her hand. 'I'm not feeling that way. I am that way.'

'He thinks so too, motherfucker. He's nineteen years old, he lives with his momma, he jerks off into gym socks and he's hitting my cutie-pie boxer with sucker lead hooks.'

Pillow pressed his nostril down with the heel of the glove and fired a .45 slug through the gun barrel of his nostril. 'He'll get his, don't worry.'

'Believe it when I see it. You haven't showed me anything but tempo-jab and a fuckin' reckless manner so far.' She shoved his mouthguard back in, then jammed the heel of her hand into the middle of his forehead.

The kid was feeling himself, tried out a shitty left hook into left uppercut, and Pillow gave him two body hooks and a hard jab down the pipe. The kid turned right back to Pillow, bit on the half-step feint and ate a clean one-two like it was a piece of birthday cake. Pillow saw the kid's eyes widen and he took a step back. Pillow shot the kid a wink and gave him a second to gather himself.

The rest of the round, and the five that followed, were vintage Pillow. The kid followed him around the ring, not quite able to cut him off, eating sharp jabs. Pillow skipped around on the back foot, freezing the kid with feints and slapping check hooks, occasionally stepping in on a wide right to the body.

Pillow finished out the last round landing a flush one-two-one, kissed the kid on the headgear and told him softly in his ear that his soul was beautiful and perfect, and danced over to Kim, dropping his head as if in supplication. As the headgear pulled off in a sweaty, jangling mass, Pillow looked up for approval and caught a hard forehand-backhand to the face. He grinned.

'I'm looking that good, huh?'

Kim gave about a quarter of a slanted smile. 'All right, Pillow. All right.'

6.

Gently schooling a man over a decade younger and twenty-five pounds heavier than himself had given Pillow a fleeting feeling of inner peace. And, as such, he and Sherlock Holmes were having a more sedate evening than usual. Sherlock was in his lounge chair reading the paper, legs crossed at the knee in a perfect bony T. Pillow splayed out across the floor tugging ineffectually at his adductors.

In his youth, Pillow had been, by whatever confusing combination of coercion and intense personal drive churns around in children who are training to be fighters, a follower of regimens. Anything he was told to do, in a day, in a week, until his body ran out of talent, he would do it without question. And he thought he liked it.

But treating every day the same only works for so many thousands of days. After regimes stopped working, Pillow went looking for new ways to make himself do the starving and self-harm required of any professional fighter. What he'd hit on was a principle of momentum. He'd had a great day in sparring, which set him up for a great night at home, which would set him up for another good day at the gym, and on and on. Lean into the good momentum and switch it up when it's going the other way.

So, tonight Pillow took only the home-brewed drugs Sherlock had made that turned his red blood cells into glowing flying saucers. He was happy on the ground, thinking about what his body was doing to itself and what he had done that day.

Sherlock was miserable in a chair thinking about what he hadn't done in many days. He puffed prissily on his pipe and spoke a disgusting-smelling word of smoke. 'CRIME!'

Pillow was low-key relieved that the guy's anxiety pot was finally boiling over. 'Say what?

Sherlock dumped his pipe and whipped the newspaper to the ground, jabbing a headline with a stiff, bone-white finger, as if Pillow was or would eventually be looking. 'Crime is ongoing, and the heights of criminal brilliance continue to be met with but the wet rag of resistance bureaucracy is capable of erecting as a wall.'

'Who's erect now?'

Holmes collapsed back in his chair, theatrically waving at the ceiling, with whom he was apparently having this conversation. 'Crimes may be important without being interesting. Indeed, the larger crimes are apt to be simpler, for the bigger the crime the more obvious, as a rule, is the motive. Bureaucracy in its best and most highly theoretical form is in the business of triage. Of deciding and acting upon only what is deemed most relevant and pressing.'

Pillow switched sides on his stretch and breathed through it. Often in a conversation, you need to signal to the other person that you're listening.

The detective swept to his feet. 'And so our public servants find themselves serving not the public, not the commons, not that which makes us humans as opposed to beasts. What separates us from beasts is but an interest in how things work, rather than the certainty to sally forward under the blunt acknowledgement that they do. Bureaucrats serve not the common store of humanity, but that which is common to the public in the area of their responsibility. A great criminal mind has been apprehended. Arsène Lupin, the master thief, has, after a series of trivial but deeply investing crimes, been arrested.'

Pillow rolled to his knees. 'So, why are you worried about crime? They got the great criminal.'

'Ah, Pillow, you have hit on what is accurate but not what is true. They "got their man," surely they did. But they do not have him. Arsène Lupin is a special breed of criminal, one upon whom

I would love to have had, or have still, the opportunity to focus my cursed gifts.' He snatched up the newspaper and waved it in Pillow's direction, still seemingly unaware that Pillow was rotating his thoracic spine at a pace and angle that made reading impossible. 'They say that, now apprehended, Lupin is being held in isolation. Isolation! As if the fire of genius could be contained by vacuum. Lupin is that nothingness. It is where he was born and into which he seeks to draw us all! To isolate this man is a terrible mistake. A loss for the science of crime and understanding and … and … '

'Justice?'

'Bah, justice! I speak of a thing past justice, which is art and soul!'

'But you said his shit was minor, right?'

'Minor in the eyes of the law, but major in the eyes of intellect. Lupin is a burglar committed to method. To the fostering of a vacuum of meaning. A man who knows the artifice inherent to all complexity. His crimes are vast cauldrons of delicately layered soup, which boil down always to a thin skim of residual fat. Lupin, you see, is the master of the signal. Of gaming a system that seeks to connect signal with noise. And in his expert working of the workings of state, he shows us the noise we make for ourselves when we fail to treat signals as what they are, which is always and only themselves first.'

Pillow hopped to his feet and grabbed his friend around the shoulders. 'Sherlock. When I was a kid, I used to bite my arm. Every day, I came home from school, and I'd go to my room and I'd whack myself in the head, I'd pinch my face, I'd bite myself. I'd beat the shit out of myself. And then do you know what I did?'

'You received psychological help for your childhood emotional problems?'

'I stopped going to my room after school.'

'Ah.'

'Go the fuck outside. Play a sport. Let's go, make it happen.'

'Pillow, while I appreciate your practical advice, I think you are missing … '

Pillow lifted Holmes over his shoulder and started toward the back door. 'You're depressed and you feel like you're missing out on your old life, blah, blah, blah.' He dropped Holmes in the yard and closed the door on him, like a clingy dog. Pillow tapped the glass in front of the detective's chest. 'Your old life isn't coming back. You get good money to make great dope. Gimme thirty push-ups.'

'There are few men whom I would permit this level of personal imposition.'

'Come on, I'll bang 'em out with you.'

Holmes eyed him for a second and smiled. 'There is truth, too, in energy.'

The two men smiled through the glass door and gave each other thirty.

7.

Pillow's favourite animals at the zoo were the giraffes. He'd do his diligence: check in with the wolf pack, pop by the weirdly humid Oceania dome with the silent room where you're not supposed to scare the kangaroo, stand at the railing and wonder how you'd feel about your skin if it was spread out as armour plates all over your body as he watched a rhinoceros take a shit. The longest visit was always with the giraffes. He'd watch them play, kick their balls around, lope toward a fake tree and eat real bananas off fake branches. The giraffes weren't just a long-neck-wow-that-really-could-be-an-alien-but-is-just-from-real-life gimmick to Pillow, either. They had more personality than the other animals. A certain style.

Pillow had named the best giraffe Gentleman Jim, even though he'd known before he named her that she was female. She wasn't a tall giraffe, but she had this erect posture, her head tilted back toward her hind. She'd stand back from the other giraffes and watch, sometimes casting a glance out toward the people. Gentleman Jim was the perfect name for her, giraffe vaginas aside.

It's hard to know how often other people are going to the zoo, but Pillow was sure he was a top-five regular. When he wasn't in camp, he made it at least once a week. And even in camp, he'd get out there twice a month. This time, he was glad to have a bonus reason for coming: Jean Painlevé was working on a movie about vampire bats, and the zoo was letting him shoot in the habitat.

Painlevé was loosely affiliated with Gwynn Apollinaire, Pillow's long-time financial backer. Apollinaire had set him up a few years ago with Painlevé, who soon became Pillow's cutman/witch doctor/exotic animal consultant. When he wasn't randomly servicing fighters with sketchy medical services, Painlevé did his own thing making nature documentaries. But nature documentaries are expensive, which made it both easy and necessary for Painlevé to do odd jobs and launder cash for Apollinaire's operation through the crazy budgets of his movies. More recently, Painlevé had convinced Pillow to get rid of his pets, which was a difficult enough thing to arrange that the little Frenchman felt obliged to help.

Gentleman Jim was standing perfectly still, her giant giraffe chin tucked back looking at the beach ball at her feet as if she had a human digestive tract and the ball was questionably cooked chicken. Pillow didn't look up when he sensed Painlevé slide onto the bench beside him. There wasn't any need to. Painlevé looked like a guy who didn't look like much and didn't think much about it. Gentleman Jim was standing so still that Pillow wondered if she was blinking.

'So, what's this big news?'

Pillow heard and saw the sidelong blur of Painlevé clapping his hands twice. 'I have finally secured a safe and caring home for Rigoberto the shark.'

Pillow was not as surprised as he should have been that Painlevé had somehow forgotten to take off his night-vision goggles. The boxer gently moved them up to the little Frenchman's forehead.

Painlevé blinked and shook his head. 'Wow, no wonder my retinas feel so crispy.'

'You didn't notice?'

'I assumed my eyes hadn't adjusted … '

'To being blinded.'

Painlevé grinned. 'To the blinding beauty of another day's sun.'

'Where's Rigoberto going?'

A quick wince and a sprightly hop to standing. 'Nowhere yet. This sanctuary is in Belgium, and while the sanctuary itself is perfectly gentle and sanctioned, moving the shark over the borders and seas required is … fraught.'

'Which is why we're not talking about this on the phone.'

'Correct. We need to get creative on this one.'

Gentleman Jim took one step backwards, as if to load up, and then rooted herself to the ground. 'I need to do right by my pets, that's all.'

'Next steps, I'll call Mr. Wilk back and inform him of your interest, and we can arrange for a meeting to hash out the details and for him to inspect the animal. And then it'll be done.'

Pillow nodded, and something somewhere in his neck snapped and grinded like an axel falling off a wagon headed to Oregon a very long time ago.

Gentleman Jim kicked the basketball over the far-side fence, sending it free of the zoo, arcing slowly toward a fading daylight's horizon it could never reach.

8.

'Are you a lover or a fighter, Pillow?'

It was a boring question asked by an interesting person, so Pillow gave it two seconds of legitimate thought. 'Neither. I'm a hot guy who loves to fight.'

Genevieve Hamon gave him a small nod, then she lifted the corner of one of the sea-horse belt buckles she was showing him. 'This is the one. For a hot guy.' She picked up the belt buckle and walked it over to her work table to wrap it.

Pillow had left Painlevé blinking out his eyes by the giraffe pen and driven straight to the little Frenchman's estate to meet the little Frenchman's wife for an appointment to buy some custom jewellery and vibe sexually.

Genevieve and Painlevé were a working couple. They collaborated in keeping Painlevé's aquarium and making movies, and Genevieve designed hipster jewellery and screen prints and ran the business, which, along with the money laundering, is what kept the doors open.

She talked to him over her shoulder casually, like she was spitballing about what groceries to buy. And, for just a second, Pillow allowed himself to feel like he was a person who a plain and lovely woman who made art every single day would talk to about groceries. 'So, you want to change the design? It'll cost a bit extra.'

Genevieve was making Pillow's custom trunks and walkout robe for the fight. Originally, he'd wanted a print of a tiger making friends with a groundhog, but the other day he'd changed his mind. 'No problem. I'll pay whatever.'

She finished wrapping the buckle and turned halfway to face him, her hip leaning a little into the desk. 'What are you thinking, then?'

'I want a giraffe. So, the giraffe is standing up but her neck is drooping over and her head is resting on a pillow. And I want her to be sleeping but smiling. Smiling in her sleep.'

'That's a fairly specific idea.'

'Can you do it?'

'Of course. No problem at all. I'll make you some other options as well. It's the curse of the consumer to get what you want and realize that all there is to want is to look like the shit you are.' She picked up the wrapped belt buckle, and Pillow walked over to take it from her. She pulled it back as he reached for it and wagged it at him a couple times. 'Now, before I give you this, I have to check something.'

'What's that?'

'Do you actually own a belt for this buckle?'

'Like a leather belt?'

'Yes. A belt for pants.'

'That's a great question. I have, obviously, championship belts.'

She gave the full impression of an eye roll with a slight tilt of her head. 'So, you've said.'

Pillow had not bought any of his own non-exercise clothes. 'Let's bet that I do.'

She flipped the wrapped buckle up and he caught it. 'Wager accepted. I'll put it on your tab.'

Pillow probably needed to take an Epsom salt bath then sleep. Pillow definitely wanted to hang out into the early morning and be watched having rough sex by sea creatures. And how can you even compare a probable need and a definite want?

He loomed behind the little Frenchman's wife and bit the top of her ear. 'You still working on that movie?'

Genevieve was packing up the rest of her accessories in a beautiful fishing basket. She folded it back together from the sides. 'I'm working on four movies. I assume you're asking about the jellyfish.' Pillow nodded, and Genevieve hooked a thumb toward the aquarium hall. 'I'll join you momentarily. Don't touch anything.'

The Painlevé/Hamon aquarium wasn't open to the public for viewings, so there weren't any chairs. There was just a giant tank full of jellyfish in the middle of an empty room. Pillow sat down in front of the tank, looking up at the glowing jellyfish wiggling around. After a couple minutes, Genevieve silently joined him. And then they sat, watching the tank, as Genevieve drank a huge, incredibly elaborate cocktail and Pillow drank water out of his gallon jug, and he learned about how some jellyfish are born.

9.

After an interval that would have felt suspicious to anyone who cared to look for meaning in time, Pillow got home. Gwynn Apollinaire appeared, looking like a statue come to life. Apollinaire was an independent gangster of the old school whose nationality was best described as Pan-European. An ancient, bone-forward woman who smoked a pack a day and told you that olive oil was the key to health. A crime boss thirty years in the game, and still smiling, still having fun, still doing it with style. She'd backed Pillow since early in his career, covering his training expenses before he was making big purses, taking her percentage and betting it on him.

As a boxer, it's common practice to get staked by some kind of low-life, whether they're a straight-up gangster or just a small-business tyrant who owns some Dollar Slice franchises, and it doesn't matter which one you get. At some point, unless you're just Mike-Ass-Tyson, your backer ends up wanting to take the short money. They set you up an easy fight with a jobber, and then they put a fat bet in on the jobber by KO. You go down when they tell you to. It's a tale as old as Roman gladiators, and as a fighter you just have to be happy combat sports have evolved and your backer's cash-out ends up with you lying down for ten seconds instead of getting eaten by a lion.

Pillow was both a romantic and a down-and-dirty realist, so from the day she started backing him he'd been waiting. Waiting for her to walk into the dressing room, give him a fat envelope full of cash, and tell him it wasn't his night. This wasn't his locker room and the fight wasn't for another month and a half, but Gwynn Apollinaire had showed up. She threw that fat envelope on the table and sat down on the arm of Pillow's giant couch.

'Do you know what that's for?'

Pillow played with the surgical scar on his right hand for a while. 'I can guess.'

Gwynn nodded sadly and started to traverse the couch. She patted his cold, damp hand with her warm, dry one, shaking her head sadly. She raised Pillow's hand to her mouth and licked the webbing between his index and middle fingers. They both laughed and she slapped him happily on the shoulder.

'Ah Pillow, I'm just tugging on your clit a little. That's your share from Sherlock's last shipment. You'll be very happy, I'm sure.'

Pillow was not quite as relieved as he should have been. He wouldn't feel like a real pro until he took a dive. But it was foolish to do it for no reason. 'I appreciate it. I really do, but I can't lie, money doesn't make me happy. I'm like, "Okay, here's some money," but it doesn't mean much in my feelings.'

She scooted back down the couch and crossed her legs elaborately. 'Here I am, Pillow. A person with ten little toes and, depending on the day, five to seven little senses, knowing of life and death what the living may know. I can speak a few languages, am pretty well-travelled. One time I was hungry for ten years. And another time I got shot in the head. So, I've got a little advice for you.'

'I could use it.'

'Expectation is always violent.'

Pillow thought about it for a second. 'In my game, so's patience.'

Gwynn clapped and jumped to her feet. 'And that's why I will bet on you until the money runs dry. Until I've turned an ocean into a desert, I will bet on you, sweet Pillow. And this time, I'm getting great odds.'

'I'm what, five-to-one underdog?'

'Line moved to five and a half today – word out of your camp is that you're unfocused.' She waggled her eyebrows at him. Thick, black ones looking like loose logs on a calm sea. 'Now, show me to my friend.'

She looped her arm out, and they walked, arm in arm, to the boxer's other living room where he kept the shark.

10.

Rigoberto the shark was proving more difficult to rehome than Jersey Joe, a little bit because ethical shark care is punishingly expensive, and another little bit because sharks are an objectively worse animal than sloths. Basically, the thing didn't really have a way to experience happiness aside from tearing another being apart. So, a lot of your more ethical, kind-hearted aquariums and animal centres aren't big on sharks. Pillow found Rigoberto boring but a great party favour. Everybody loved to see the shark, especially women, which surprised Pillow. He'd thought they would like the gentle, cuddly sloth better, and he'd been wrong only because he'd only ever been with women who wanted to fuck a boxer.

Gwynn was watching the shark paddle aimlessly around his tank. She smiled. 'The other day, I had a dream that I was a house in the middle of the sea. And the windows of me the house were rivers, flowing out of my eyes. And the walls were octopi, and all you could hear were each of their three heartbeats, and the echo you only get in water.'

'The other day I had a dream that I ate a slice of cake and gained fourteen pounds. That's maybe a bit less whimsical and shit.'

'What we lose in whims we gain in shit. And only one of those two things is edible.' Gwynn nodded and waved vaguely, and to Pillow it seemed like air should just move right through the thin skin of her hand. As if it hadn't touched anything. If air even ever does touch anything. 'All right, Pillow, let's talk turkey.'

'I have nothing to say about dry meat, Gwynn. I talk boxing.'

'So, how much should I bet on you? I'm asking seriously.'

Pillow answered before she was done talking. 'Everything that's not tied down.'

'Really, you're motivated?'

'I'll tell you this, I'm a month and a half out. In training I'm dragging ass. At home I'm doing everything wrong …

'Hence the cake dreams.'

'Hence all over that shit. Hence as all get-out. By the time I fight, I will be undertrained, barely motivated, and more than slick enough to hand this basic bitch hype job his ass in a paper bag and convince him it's thirteen bagels. Cannot lose. Bet everything that's not tied down.'

Gwynn checked him out in her peripheral vision, pretending to still be looking at the shark. 'I don't know if I can bet on someone who isn't having fun. It's against my principles.'

Pillow jolted back, hit a pivot, and reeled some uppercuts. Rigoberto approached the back limit of his tank and lazily turned around, then he opened his giant scary mouth for no reason at all. 'In that ring, I have fun all day.' He stopped throwing punches but kept up a bounce from one leg to the other. 'I hate it, but fighting is fun as shit. Bet it all.'

Gwynn stilled him by grabbing his shoulder, then she looked back at the tank. 'I believe you. But, as a show of solidarity, maybe I take that envelope of yours and lay it down for you? Bet on yourself, as a rich American would tell a poor one.'

'Hell yes, bet that and the next one. I'll remortgage this house and bet that. Whatever odds you can get, bet it all. There are no odds for infinity, baby. I win this fight every time, and I look beautiful every time I win.'

Gwynn was back on that eyebrow game.

Pillow thought the whole thing over for one legitimate minute. 'I had a coach when I was a kid. And he told me that to train a dog, to make him listen always, when he shits on the carpet as a puppy you don't yell or hit him with a newspaper. No bad-dog bullshit. You get down on the ground, take him in your arms, coo in his little face, pet him twice, then slap him as hard as you can. That is what a dog remembers. Pet, pet, slap. If you want to train someone, a dog, an opponent, whoever, that's the way to do it. Pet, pet, slap. That was school for me. That's what I learned, what I was taught about life. About what life's like.'

They stood there awhile, watching the shark sway around the tank, a flickering green glow on their faces. Gwynn squeezed Pillow's forearm.

'Is this the last one? The last fight?'

Pillow smiled, stepped forward and tapped the glass. Rigoberto didn't notice, or, if he did, didn't care. He kept swimming because that's what sharks have to do not to die.

II.

It was true that Pillow was acting like a lazy shithead this camp. It was also true that Pillow did not act any kind of way for no reason. And the big truth sitting on top of all the other truths was just that his hand hurt. His right hand hurt every day. It hurt when he hit the bag, it hurt when he sparred. It hurt at home and at the gym. It hurt when the sky dreamed about rain.

Pillow's start in boxing had been smooth. He learned his fundamentals, he worked hard, and all he did was box and think about boxing. He stopped taking the bus and just ran everywhere. He had this little backpack that he could fit a shirt and jeans in, and he ran everywhere he went. He'd run to the gym and whoop somebody, learn something new, run home.

That was how it went for years. He started fighting youth amateurs right away. Won a few tournaments, then turned pro at eighteen. And every second of the day, he was winning. And he'd been right in the middle of winning his seventh pro fight when he landed a right hook on the guy's elbow and his fourth metacarpal crumbled like a very tall, very rotten tree.

There was the plate they put in to hold his hand together, then the tendon repair after his hand moved and the plate didn't, then the spot where the bone sheared away from the plate, then there was taking the plate out and replacing it with some of his hip bone. And always, every time something happened and all the time in between, his hand hurt every different way something can. It ached, it swelled, it stabbed, it shocked. And now, nothing was easy. Nothing was easy except the jab.

Pillow had always been a cutie-pie boxer, happy to fight off the back foot, look pretty making the other guy miss. Once the hand went, so did whatever had existed of his power. For an outside fighter, it's the rear hand that backs the opponents off.

The cross that straightens them up, the uppercut that catches them coming in. Those times you plant your feet and get some respect. And, for Pillow, that was gone. He still threw his right hand, but never at full power. He'd slap with it or pull it. He'd fire it from the shoulder, good enough to score but no body weight behind it. Before he broke the hand, he'd knocked out four of his first seven opponents. Four KOs in a year. In the decade after that, he'd stopped one guy, and that guy had quit on the stool.

A great lie sounds exactly like a hard truth. Pillow had been telling a great lie: that the real battle of hand problems is mental. He'd said your hand can be perfect, but if you're used to training one-handed your brain will catch you, stop you throwing it with the full power that you do, in fact, have. And everyone had believed him, because it sounded like a difficult thing to admit. But there was nothing to admit other than his hand hurt every day. It hadn't been fixed for a second. So, even if Pillow had felt motivated, if he'd still loved the game, if it had still been more than a paycheque, he wouldn't have been able to train the right way.

The cruellest part about the end of a boxer's career is that the gap between what you know and what you can do only keeps growing, and it grows from both ends. You get older and you learn more and you see more. You start to understand the fine details and you have more ideas about the big-picture strategy. And all the time you're seeing these new angles, you're getting slower. You're seeing openings you never would have seen as a kid, but you need to be as fast as you were then to use them.

Pillow knew how to beat Julio Solis. Dance the whole time, full energy. Every trick in the book, every feint. Keep the kid from setting his feet. Tire him out, then walk him down in the late rounds. Pillow could see it in his mind, but he also knew what it would feel like to do, how much wind it would take. How strong his legs would have to be, how many right hands hard enough to kill a full-grown Doberman he'd have to eat with a smile on his face, asking for more.

At the gym, Pillow pushed air out of his body in a very specific way and wondered what animals thought plants were as a 'roided-to-the-tits assistant trainer everyone called Sheep Dog hit him 100 times in the tummy with a medicine ball.

Pillow's best non-boxing skill was giving people nicknames. Everyone on staff, everyone in Kim's stable, had a nickname, and everyone's nickname had come from Pillow. There was 'Toe Shoe' Terry Moylan, a tall middleweight with prehensile toes; there was 112-pound belt holder Guillermo Perez, 'Big Dick' Billy P. A thick-bottomed super middleweight called Stacks. As with everything he was good at, Pillow had a complex system supporting his nick-naming that he would do a very poor job of explaining if anyone asked about it. There was a slick balance to the nickname game. For starters, a good nickname is never mean, otherwise you're a bully. On the other hand, a good nickname can never be too flat-tering or the person won't want to use the nickname or, if they do, is an asshole. The nickname can't be too straight on. You can't nickname a guy with a harelip Harelip Steve. As with everything Pillow knew about, the nickname game is about angles. A good nickname comes from the inside angle, just off-centre, but close enough to feel true.

And that was how he'd hit on his nickname masterpiece: his own. A lot of boxers give themselves nicknames, and almost always those nicknames are pure trash. One Punch. Sweet Hands. Kid Dynamite. The Executioner. Pillow had started introducing himself as Pillow Fist just before everyone started talking about how pillow-fisted he was. He'd introduce himself as Pillow Fist, and people would squint at him, and then he'd wrap them around the shoulders, say, 'Pillow for short.' And from then on, a lot of people who would have thought he was a mobbed-up piece of shit had a certain weird, automatic affection for him. A nickname takes you from cheating criminal disgrace to adorable rascal real quick. Right off the bat, a great nickname makes everyone feel a little bit like they made it up. Like they're in on something with you before they're done shaking your hand. Pillow didn't know if Big Dick Billy P really had a big dick, but that's the truth of a nickname.

Probably, animals don't think plants are anything in particular. Probably, because when they're smart it's a whole other kind of smart, animals don't spend a lot of time thinking about what other things are, only whether or not they're edible or dangerous, and then just about how to eat those things or run away from them. Animals probably aren't spending too much time playing the name game with themselves. The next medicine ball strike came in slightly off-centre and caught Pillow's floating rib and, because he was a professional, Pillow responded to the searing pain by closing one eye and smiling slightly.

Kim whooped. 'Give it to him, Sheep Dog, give it to him raw.'

Pillow kept his eyes trained on the ball and flipped her off.

Kim lay down on ground next to Pillow's face and pounded the canvas with an open hand. 'Give it to him raw and bust a fat one, baby. Let's see my star ath-uh-lete waddle to the bathroom like a gentleman.'

Sheep Dog gave Pillow ten more with the medicine ball, then tucked the ball between his arm and ribs, the place where most people have an armpit and where Sheep Dog just kept some of the extra lats he had lying around. Sheep Dog went for a fist bump and Pillow grazed the bottom of his knuckles and did a brief mental survey of his internal organs while he got his breath back.

Kim wagged a finger at him like she was bouncing it off an overinflated balloon. 'I'll give it to you. You ain't in shape, but you sure can tank those body shots.'

Finally feeling confident that he could move without shitting himself, Pillow rolled onto his knees and settled into the version of child's pose that what he had left of his knee cartilage allowed.

He took a deep breath and eventually got standing up straight. It wasn't so much that he had a cramp in his abs as his entire being was a cramp.

He could feel Kim eyeballing and deciding something. She popped back to her feet in a boxing stance, bouncing and shuffling around the ring. 'All right, all right, buttercup. Turn around.' She settled her weight into her legs, then tightened up into a rigid, hand-up stance. 'We been busting your body, let's start thinking this thing through.'

The cramp was starting to subside a little. Pillow bounced on his toes, hoping to loosen up a little. 'Start? I got this puff-piece all broken down already. Who's the trainer here?'

Kim did a picture-perfect impression of Solis tapping his forehead with his glove on the reset. 'The one who makes sure you don't embarrass your profession, that's who the trainer is.' She did a quick forward bounce and a long step back. 'See, that's the only feint he'll give you. He's slick on the straight lines … '

Pillow slipped an imaginary right hand.

Kim moved in closer. As she hit the edge of range, she flashed an open palm and Pillow snapped a jab into it. Rather than cutting him off, she moved past him on a line as he sidestepped, flashed the other palm, and caught Pillow's soft right with it. 'See, the reason I'm busting on you is … ' She flashed forward with both palms and caught Pillow's combo before he circled out. 'You can beat this motherfucker's ass, bad, but to do it, you need the legs. SPRAWL.'

Pillow sprawled, popped up, and reeled off a dozen shoe-shining uppercuts. He bounced on his toes while Kim grabbed her mitts from the ring apron.

She marched back over to him and put a hand on each of his shoulders. 'You need those legs *strong*.' She pushed with full force down on Pillow's shoulders, making him dip low and take a step back to steady himself, then she popped forward in her Solis impression again. 'He's stiff, he's green, he's made for you. But the right hand is legit. And, if you really want to kick his ass, you've got to get low. I'm talking butt to heel, son. We get you low in your stance, make him punch down. We give him the angles side to side with the feet, and we give it to him up and down, changing levels.'

Pillow dropped low in his stance, and Kim threw an exaggerated downward jab, then flashed her palms for him to reel off another combo.

'He's robotic, and a robot can never be smart. They just repeat smart shit they've been told. He knows you want to dance on him. He knows you're going to give him angles, right? If you give him the footwork side to side *and* you can siddown and move him up and down at the same time, that's money. Do your thing on the outside, do you, but once in a while, when he squares up trying to cut you off, you're going to shield up, get inside, and dig to the body. Not trading with him but working and getting out. Get your shit off, frame out. Right, we slip the jab, we don't try to run, we duck, let him fall over the front foot on that right hand, then slide. Slip, duck, slide, hooks to the body. All night.'

It was a perfect game plan. Pillow knew it the way a giraffe knows the taste of tree fruit.

Kim launched forward, held both pads up, and let him reel off straight punches bare-handed into the mitts. 'We got the medicine for this kid, Pillow. We got the medicine. Just give me you, man. The real you training hard and you bust his ass wide open. And why?'

Pillow felt his pace picking up, and he picked it up again, double time.

'Because you're the motherfucking truth, and he's a guess.'
Pillow threw sixteen uppercuts.
'Because he was made and you were born.'
Pillow threw twelve hooks.

'Because he thinks he knows.'

Pillow threw twenty-five uppercuts.

'Because he thinks he can know.'

Pillow threw thirty straight punches.

'Because you got what everyone wants.'

Pillow threw forty more straight punches, dropped, and did a push-up for free.

'Because you're my motherfucking trillion-dollar, thinks-on-its-own NASA boxing computer, and he's a laptop.'

Pillow popped up and reeled off his last twenty punches, closing with a hard right hand that stung all the way up to his shoulder, then spun on his heel and marched to the edge of the ring, shouting at the top of his lungs.

'Because fuck the moon.'

12.

Having finally strung a few decent training sessions together, Pillow had been given a legitimate rest day, so he wasn't thrilled to open his eyes and see Sherlock Holmes sitting cross-legged on his bed. Holmes began talking as if he and Pillow were in the middle of a conversation.

'You see, dear Pillow, that I am in the uncomfortable position of being a man in the habit of observation. The beautiful and occasionally troublesome thing about habits is that after a time they gain a power of their own. An independence from the conventions and principles guiding and propelling the vehicle of one's life. For instance, a thing I hold dear is the intimate confidence between lodgers.'

Pillow knew where this was going, so he spun his hand around to signal for Sherlock to keep talking, then rubbed the back of the hand bluntly over, around, and into his eyeball.

'The confidences of rooming bachelors are sacred things, as you know, for they are both discretely and willingly given and passively but firmly held. There are the things told and spoken of only under conditions of intimacy, and there are the things seen and spoken of never, to anyone. Sadly, the habit of my circumstance, and very possibly my nature, have accustomed me to draw conclusions from that which I see, and having gained an abiding affection for you from all you have freely revealed to me, I am obliged to warn you of the conclusions obvious from that which I have chanced to observe within the bounds of our shared space.'

Pillow sat up and closed one eye, then the other, alternating like that for a bit. It helped with the double vision. 'So, what're you going to tell me here, Sherlock?'

Holmes nodded sort of sidelong, patting Pillow on the calf. 'From my mere presence in this room at this moment, I can deduce that your adductors are feeling uncommonly limber this morning and that you are considering a trip to China after your next contest.'

Pillow rubbed a piece of sleep out of his eye that was as hard, pointy, and large as a very cheap diamond. 'Listen, if you're going to jerk off in my room, just please don't make a mess.'

Sherlock paused and arched an eyebrow. 'Upon entering your room, I observed four seemingly disparate objects of note. One, your passport, strewn across your bed. It does not take a detective of my calibre to deduce that you were looking at the aforesaid passport, possibly to check that it is still valid, and then to peruse the stamps, reflecting on your past trips. For a man of your active character, this signals to me a vision of future plans rather than a purely nostalgic rumination. The other object of note is the strap hanging from the head of your marble lion in the corner. The lion stands, proudly, in his empty corner, which, having noted the scuffing and marking of the wood in this area, has been kept clear of other furniture for use as an area for stretching and light calisthenics to be undertaken in the morning and, in cases of anxiety, before you retire.'

'How do you know I'm anxious?'

'That evidence was not so much in the room as in the fact that I live in your home and prepare vast amounts of benzodiazepine bio-equivalents for you on a weekly basis.'

'What a detective.'

'Continuing on, to the two objects which connect the lot, those being the loose cotton pants and white tank top strewn across the lip of your laundry hamper. Judging by their residual dampness, one can conclude that these must have been employed as exercise clothes within the last twelve hours; however, the heaviness and cotton base of the pants renders them a particularly unintuitive and impractical set of exercise clothes, especially to a man as evidently attentive to the benefits of exercise tights as yourself.' The detective shifted his eyes to Pillow's open closet, which was a very long hallway half full of absurdly expensive dress shirts and drab workout gear, then he chucked a thumb in the direction of the tights Pillow'd left on the floor beside the hamper. 'So, the only logically coherent and non-idiotic conclusion to draw is that last evening after your training you vapourized an inadvisable amount of THC and watched footage of stylized martial combat from the Orient. Feeling appropriately inspired, you decided to remove your tights, replacing them with the loose cotton pants you bought specifically because they resemble those of Chinese martial artists. You then continued stretching, feeling all the while a strong urge to train kung-fu "for real," and you responded to this urge by making a mental plan to visit a Shaolin temple after your fight. The only step in furtherance of which you took was to peruse your passport. Bringing us once more into the cyclical, recursive harmony of logic and the rhythm of life itself.'

'Sure, man. You also just know I'm into Bruce Lee.'

'It is true, Pillow, that the more valuable and profound knowledge is that which I have of your character. I know what I see around you, but I know you better, Pillow. And I know you don't think about other places or long-dead martial artists unless you are in a place you no longer wish to be, doing things in a way you no longer wish to be doing them. And from this I may reason quite definitively that you have lost patience with yourself, Pillow. And that it is making you very sad.'

Pillow laughed. He gestured at the giant framed portrait of Jersey Joe the sloth oozing across the front gate. 'No shit. How'd you know I hit the adductors?'

Sherlock scratched his sharp nose with a dull fingernail. 'Because you rose to sit in a lotus pose.'

Pillow looked down at the walled courtyard of his own groin and snorted. 'Elementary.'

Sherlock clapped. It sounded like two sticks of bamboo being smashed together. 'As always, my man, it is I both introducing a topic and following your premise. I admit my own contribution to the staid air of this house. The arrest of Lupin and ego's tug on the leash of my pride have been oppressing me.'

'Sorry, quick question: why do you care? You're retired. The world keeps spinning.'

'The continued rotation of this planet is a fact with little bearing on the emotional environment of this household, and, like any such physical truth, is true only and exactly until it is no longer so. Why do I care … ?'

Holmes stared into the middle distance for longer than socially comfortable, then shot his finger up to point to the ceiling. 'Regardless of its origins, we find ourselves beset by a pestilence of the spirit. It is, however, nothing to offer a diagnosis without a cure. The prescription, sir, is energy!' Holmes stood dramatically and whipped off Pillow's sheets. Neither of them were remotely fazed by how nude he was, nor by how spongily engorged his morning penis still was. 'You have the day off from training, correct?'

'Correct.'

'Excellent, for today we shall treat the malaise that has infected this house. Arsène Lupin is forgotten! A game is afoot.'

Pillow stood and grabbed sweatpants and a zip-up hoodie with a faux-fur hood. 'A foot's a foot.'

The doorbell rang. Holmes grinned. 'And there's our client.'

13.

The woman at the door was nicely dressed in a perfectly neutral way. She wore a black skirt, a clean white blouse, and no jewellery. A real cutie, to Pillow's eye. Real in that she was both truly cute and real in that she seemed like a real person with a job and so forth. She had a great head of hair on her, flowing in these long coils down her shoulders, styled the way they do an actress's to make you think she's just a regular person with incredible hair. It was eye-catching enough to make Pillow's hand drift unconsciously to the ratty tips of his own hair, which reminded him and made him so, so regretful of the fact that he was wearing sweatpants and a wide open hoodie with a faux-fur hood.

The cutie eyed him skeptically for a second and focused on Sherlock, who she obviously recognized. 'Hi, so I'm … '

'Miss Violet Hunter. Pleased to make your acquaintance. Follow me as I welcome you into a living room that is not my own.'

Sherlock ushered her in, and before everyone sat down, gestured ganglily at Pillow. 'Miss Hunter, allow me to introduce to you my trusted colleague and flat-, or I should say mansion-mate, Peter Wilson, he goes by Pillow.'

Pillow smoothly swooped in beside Violet Hunter and extended his hand. 'Nice to meet you.'

She shook his hand as firmly as her tiny hand allowed, looked him over skeptically, and sat down.

Sherlock continued, 'Anything you say to me, you may say in front of Pillow; he is my colleague in the fullest sense of the word. Presently, I shall ask that you recount the details of the case that led you to send me your missive. But first I must ask how your note came to find me. Since I am, to the public's knowledge, deceased.'

She smiled. 'Doctor Watson says hi.'

Sherlock slapped the thin slices of skin and pant covering his kneecaps. 'Scoundrel. Well, I am sure you are aware, then, of the accuracy of the trust I place in my colleagues. Please, tell us of the details of your situation.'

She took a deep breath and looked down at her lap for the first time. 'I'm sorry, I know that this … I know this is obviously rinky-dink to you, but I don't have parents or any relatives who I could ask for this kind of advice … And, well, I just hope you can tell me what to do in this spot.'

Pillow could see that Holmes liked her off the bat. He was already leaned back in his chair with his actually-paying-attention face, fingers tented out in front of him. 'I shall be happy to do whatever I can to assist you.'

She looked up and nodded. 'Okay then. So, I'm a teacher by trade. And, it's … it's like an apocalypse job market right now, so for the last couple years I've been working privately, homeschooling for a family and subbing when I can. Unfortunately, the family I had a steady gig with, the father's in the Navy and he got transferred to Halifax, Nova Scotia, and, I am not moving to Halifax, Nova Scotia. So, I've been looking for a job, burning through my savings, and, uh, it's getting pretty dark. Like, going-to-an-educational-job-matching-agency dark … '

Pillow had been watching her breathing, and seeing her breath catch he jumped in. 'You want a water?'

She blew out a full breath and sat up straighter. 'Yeah, actually. Yes, please.'

'Are you quick?'

She shot him a quizzical half smile. Pillow was pretty sure they'd be flirting if she wasn't clearly in distress. Without telegraphing it at all, Pillow flipped the formerly frozen bottle of water he'd used to ice his plantar fascia from under the couch toward her in a loose arc.

She caught the bottle and shook it at him before taking a drink that was obviously quite a bit bigger than she'd intended and panic-gulping it down. She gathered herself and screwed the cap back on. 'That was a slow toss, so you didn't even find out.'

Holmes cleared his throat. 'I would surmise, Miss Hunter, that your banter proves a speed more than ample to have gained Pillow's esteem.'

Violet Hunter was blushing a little now. She took a more discreet sip of the water. 'I'm sorry to waste time, but this whole thing is so weird. Anyway, I'm with this supposedly great agency, and they've been finding me exactly nothing for months now. Then, last week they call me in, and there's not just the agency lady, there's also this guy. I was a little … whatever that he was there, because you're not supposed to meet the employers before you've expressed interest, but the guy was … I don't know, he was just so smiley and … stout. Like, that's weird to say but he just had a good, happy vibe, I don't mean to get off … '

'I assure you, Miss Hunter, that once I consent to hear a tale, I prefer and require all details that come to mind, regardless of their seeming relevance.'

She nodded and took another sip. 'Okay, they call me in, I meet the guy, and he seems cool. He asks me if I'm "looking for a situation," which sounds creepy but did not register that way in the moment. He asks about my credentials, and he asks what I was making with my last family. I tell him I was getting $2,500 a month to home-school three elementary kids. And he acts like that's a crazy number, and he does this whole speech about how either I'm qualified to school and train and raise up a child who is going to be a – what'd he say? a child who will "play a part in history" is what he says – he says either I'm qualified or I'm not, and if I'm qualified then I deserve no less than six figures for the year, and he offers me a $100,000 salary to move to the townships there, live on-site, and teach his kid.'

Holmes untented his hands and cracked them. 'A most investing proposal.'

'Yeah, yes. I mean, I was … I'm so broke that I couldn't even believe it, and I guess I just looked stunned or whatever, because he pulls out a chequebook, signs one, and slides it over. This cheque he's written is for $50,000. He pays the high salary and he pays in advance because I have to make my own way there and pay my own moving costs, all that.' She shook her head, sipped again. 'So, it's a crazy offer, but it's through this agency, he's explaining it, and I couldn't – still can't – figure out how this would be a prank or something, but I really don't want to get, y'know, whatever, so I wanted more details before I committed.'

'A most prudent choice.'

'He tells me my duties are just to home-school and caretake one seven-year-old boy, and that's it. I develop a curriculum and teach it. I'm like "Is that all?", and this is where things get hinky, or hinkier, I guess. He says that the wife likes the house a certain way, and I don't have to do housekeeping, but I do have to keep things the way the wife likes and do what she says, basically. I ask him what kind of stuff she'd want. He says that they're "faddy people," which I guess he means trendy, I don't know. Anyhow, he says they're faddy people and if his wife asks me to wear a certain colour or a dress, would I be willing to wear it?'

Pillow blurted: 'Red flag.' Seeing how the other two people in the room reacted to him, he understood he'd broken the flow. 'Sherlock, I know you're the world's greatest detective, but I thought I'd just jump in to tell you that's a red flag. For hiring.'

Sherlock chuckled, then stilled his face back into blank-canvas detective mode. 'An observation, I've reason to suspect, was understood with as much clarity and substantially more subtlety by Miss Hunter, correct?'

Violet nodded and raised her eyebrows mockingly. 'Indeed, sir, you are.' She took a much deeper sip, then pulled her neck tight apologetically as she wiped water from her chin. 'Exactly. And I am not down to get sex-trafficked. At all. The thing of it is, there's no way that's how you would do it. Like, nobody is fronting $50,000 and going through an accredited agency just to pick up a random elementary educator to … y'know, do sex crimes on.'

Holmes cocked his head to the side, and Pillow could see him thinking about nicotine and manners. 'Your supposition, if not logically bulletproof, is a fair one to make.'

'Even your best logic can't take a bullet, Sherlock.'

'A wonderful observation, once again, dear Pillow. Back to your account, Miss Hunter.'

'Right, and also, I would say this guy did not give me any creepy vibes, not that that's … '

'Your impressions of the man's carriage are as valuable a data point as any other, and moreso than many.'

'Okay, so, I'm listening, and he says that also the wife would want me to have short hair. Before I start.'

Pillow shook his head and started waving his hands.

Violet Hunter nodded and pointed at him. 'Exactly. That is a creepy thing to ask, man, and it's just not cool to ask that of someone. Also, I don't want to sound whatever, but my hair is luxuriant. Straight up. It's the most consistent nice thing people say about me.'

Pillow jumped in. 'It's the best hair I've ever seen in real life. And I've met some pretty big R & B singers.'

'Thank you. It's … I mean, it's just hair, but it's … It's a big part of my self-image. Basically, it's the only thing about myself that I feel totally unambiguously good about. Is my stupid hair. So, I tell him no. That's too far for me. And he says, "Are you sure? It's my wife's demand and I can't hire someone unless they have short hair." I ask why, he just says, "Whims."'

Sherlock had gotten his pipe going as she was talking. He let a fat puff out of one side of his mouth before talking. 'I am to understand that you turned down the offer conclusively at this point?'

She remembered and fixed her posture again and took another little huffing breath to settle down. 'Yes. And I have that thing where I get home and immediately regret just, like, swallows my whole mind and body. The agency is probably going to drop me, fine whatever, but I am also broke. That $50,000 I was looking at, that pays all my debt, with some left over, and it's only half! If I do this gig for a year, I'm free and clear, with savings, for one year teaching one little kid at a rustic farm estate. Obviously, it's a sketchy situation, but I'm thinking, like, did watching eighty hours of *Law and Order: SVU* smack in the middle of puberty fuck me up for life?'

Pillow nodded. 'Honestly, it can't have been good.'

She nodded back vigorously. 'If I'm being paranoid about the weird stuff, then I turned this down for what? For my hair? It grows back. It's hair, that's all it does!' She took another calming sip, already nearing the end of the bottle. 'So, I'm in the middle of just an absolute self-hate crisis, and then I get a note. Now, he's offering me $120K, and he explains in a bit more detail that there's just this one blue dress the wife will want me to wear sometimes, and that he knows the hair thing is weird. The dress belonged to their daughter, blah, blah, and his wife has a thing about this particular dress. He says he knows it's weird, but other than this, they're going to leave me alone and let me do the job. He understands the hair is a big commitment, but it's part of the reason the offer is so high relative to the market. So, I think I just have to take it. I can't afford not to. But, before I cut my hair and move to the countryside, I thought I'd take a shot in the dark and ask you what you think of this whole thing.'

Holmes blew a small puff through his nose, then killed the pipe on his stand. 'If your mind is made up, the question is settled.'

'But you don't think I should take it?'

'I confess that it is not the situation I should like to see a sister of mine apply for.'

'What does it mean, though?'

Holmes spread his hands and shrugged. 'I have no data. What is your truest opinion?'

She slugged the last of the water, and Pillow opened his hands. She tossed the empty over to him. 'I really, truly do not think it's a sex thing. But. I think his wife is totally nuts, and even if she doesn't involve herself in my job and doesn't make me do anything but cut my hair and wear a dress, it's going to be really uncomfortable and unhealthy. Which sucks, but sucks a whole lot less than, um, abject poverty. I would just … feel better if I knew there was some backup. So, I know it's a big ask, and I've rambled forever already, but … '

Holmes stood, walked over, and kneeled in front of her, his knees cracking so loudly and viscerally that Pillow felt like he was touching the cartilage with his mind. Holmes patted the top of her hand. 'You may go forward knowing that you have not only my respect and admiration, but also my full support. If you have any reason whatsoever, even if you simply feel like it, you may contact me anytime, day or night. Although I am dead, I still have some ways of knowing and seeing, upon which I must now call to make sure I am not sending you into a situation you cannot get out of. Day or night, if you call on me I will be there as soon as I am able.'

She exhaled. 'Thank you so much. I … thank you. And I am going to take this job, and cash a $60,000 cheque, and be debt-free for the first time in my life and call you if and when it gets weird.'

Holmes stood again and nodded at her in a way that somehow fully substituted for a hug. '*If and when* is a lovely turn of phrase in this beautiful, indeterminately deterministic universe of ours.' He turned to Pillow. 'Please entertain our guest while I make the requisite arrangements for her safety.'

Pillow clicked his tongue. 'No problem, colleague.'

Holmes swept out of the room.

Violet Hunter dropped her head into her hand and rubbed her forehead for quite a while. She looked up through some shampoo-commercial coils of bang. Pillow winked as platonically as he physically could.

'My man's a lot. A real room-presence.'

'You said it. Wow. Whew, okay.'

'Take a minute for yourself. We can do a tour if you want, or we can just sit here.'

She let out another deep breath, then she looked around at the ceilings. 'Ok, I don't want to … but are you a basketball player or something?'

'I'm the something. Boxer.' He pointed at the wall behind her.

She twisted in her seat. 'Oh wow, okay.' Violet eyed the entire wall that was also a photo-realistic painting of Pillow in his boxing gloves and trunks, floating on an ocean of undulating eyeballs boxing a disintegrating clock. 'You must be good.'

'Nah, just lucky. Lucky to be good.'

'Lucky to be good, I like it. I like it.' She stood and shook out her arms and paced a couple steps.

'You like it so much, wanna come to a fight?'

'You're fighting?'

'Six weeks, yeah. At the Forum. I can get you ringside. It's fun.'

She stopped pacing and gave him some side-eye. 'You're offering me tickets?'

'I'm offering you front-row tickets, yeah. No strings, of course.'

'Oh well, if there's no strings.' She did a great imitation of herself earnestly considering something. 'Still a hard pass. Remember, I'm going to be working.'

'They'll give you the night off. As long as you wear an orange dress and shave your eyebrows or whatever.'

She laughed a tension-releasingly exaggerated amount, capped it with the slightest snort. 'I'll be honest with you, I'm pretty sure if I watched a boxing fight in person I would start crying really hard really early on.'

'It's a rough sport.'

'It's horrifying. Like, maybe the scariest and least pleasant thing I could think of.'

Pillow nodded in a sidelong way that made a couple of the disks in his neck feel good for a second. 'That's a sensible reaction. Sherlock Holmes can judge a character.'

'Mrs. Holmes raised no fools.'

'I straight up had not considered that he had parents. Shit. Mrs. Holmes, that's a fantasy dinner guest right there.'

'So, you're, like, roommates?'

'Yeah, and he helps me with my … ' It was a very unfortunate moment for him to direly need to hork phlegm up his throat, 'my supplements.'

'And you help him with cases?'

'What? It's not clear that I'm at least as observant as Sherlock Holmes?'

Violet looked at him with an immediate and comfortable skeptical eye. 'Oh, you've been ob-ser-ving plenty, buddy, but that doesn't make you observant.'

Pillow grinned, flashed the gold tooth. 'You wanna see my shark?'

14.

'Dude, this shark is … ' Violet Hunter partially closed one eye, which crinkled her whole half face in a very cute way.

'Boring and disappointing and giving off stockbroker vibes.'

'Absolutely, yes. You've … ' She looked back at the shark, then extended her fist, which Pillow bumped. 'You nailed the vibe on this shark.'

'He's my only other roommate.'

'Do people really like this? This show-them-the-shark move?'

Pillow smiled and looked over her head and then down at her whole body. Pillow had never in his life had a co-worker, but Violet was dressed the way he imagined the co-worker you have a crush on dresses. 'Some people do. I used to have a sloth, I liked him better.'

'Awwww, I would kill … '

'What? What would you kill to cuddle a sloth?'

'Oh fuck, they actually cuddle … ' She cradled her heart briefly. 'And obviously it's not a *what*, when I say I'd kill for something, I'm talking about people, I was hesitating on the number. It's six.'

'Wow, six. Sloth-loving serial killer over here.'

'It's only serial if I do all six in a ritualistic fashion, usually to derive paraphilic satisfaction. If I don't do it any particular way, for any specifically psycho reason, I'm just a sloth-loving multiple murderer.'

The tank hummed. Pillow smiled. Rigoberto bumped into the glass, and nobody bothered to look at him.

Violet shrugged. 'I'm into crime shit.'

Pillow craned his head down, trying to look Rigoberto in his dead shark eyes. 'Not me. You ask me, I say fuck crime. That's a nice thing about animals. Even this lunatic over here.' Pillow took two steps to his left, and Rigoberto tracked his movement before listing toward the back of the tank. 'He couldn't commit a crime if he wanted to, doesn't even know what a crime is. He sees shit and he does it. He smells through water.'

'Was that the end of that thought?'

Pillow grinned and turned his back on the shark, leaning his weight on the glass. 'When you think something with that level of … '

'Gravitas.'

'Sure, with that. With my gravitas, a thought never truly ends.'

Violet laughed and looked over Pillow's shoulder at the shark, moving whatever he needed to move over his gills not to die. 'It does make me like him better.'

Sherlock called Violet's name from the other room. She bobbed her eyebrows and turned to leave, and Pillow caught her wrist with his index finger.

'Hey, what say I call you sometime?'

'What say sometime had best be a time you've got a sloth to show me.'

Pillow moved his finger from her wrist to the groove in the side of his nose he touched when slightly embarrassed.

'Take it sleazy, boxerman.'

'Only way I know how.'

15.

People who do nothing but watch other people do things know a lot about how the people they watch should act and how the people they watch should feel about acting the way they should act. And, when you're a boxer as good as Pillow, they tell you about it. How much of your money you should keep. How much you should appreciate your talent. They think that when a boxer doesn't do all the things they know he should, it's always and only because the boxer is stupid.

What Pillow knew is that there are usually a whole lot of feelings that make it hard to do what you know is smart. As you're getting smarter, there are only ever more of those feelings. Because things happen. Because you get hurt. Because you get no time off. Because there's always a young kid coming up and he's coming for exactly what you have, ready to beat you to death to take it. Because people you care about take advantage of you, and it makes you feel stupid and hurt and sad and most of all confused. So, you can sit on the sidelines and ask why a boxer doesn't just save their money and, if you do that, you can be a fool for no reason other than that it's harder to know what you're talking about.

As a young man, Pillow had been given much more reason than a normal young man to feel perfect and invincible, because for a long time that's what he was. Everything he did worked perfectly, every time, and a lot of what he did was use his body to beat the best in the world. That, along with various parts of his body and mind, had cracked along the way, and he didn't feel perfect and invincible anymore. Most days, he just felt okay. Other days, he thought about all the people at the gym, and all the gyms and all the people at them, and how much of what he had they wanted and how much it hurt them to know they'd never get it. And on those days, Pillow picked up the phone and left Kim a message that he was sick and he needed another day off. He'd gone for his run, and now he had a fever, he'd say. Then, he'd go downstairs and eat a nine-egg omelette and a pound of pretzels for breakfast.

There was a room in the house that Pillow had taken to calling the Dojo, as one of those jokes that becomes an embarrassing truth almost immediately. It was an office, decorated in just about the most anti-social way possible. He'd put up slip lines across the whole room, so you had to duck just to enter. In this room, Pillow spent hours doing things that nobody else would call training: vaping, watching kung-fu movies and black-and-white boxing matches, shadowboxing, doing wushu forms, and hitting the double-end bag. Pillow still loved boxing. He just didn't love training for fights for money.

Sherlock knew that if he smelled a dry, dank vapour in the air and heard some sixties girl pop blasting, he could come right on in and get a boxing lesson. Pillow was practising a pendulum step into a darting right hand, trying to decide whether he liked the pivot out or grab-and-smother to finish. He saw Sherlock, pulled the detective in, and planted him in a boxer's stance.

In a full lather, boxing in the best rhythm he was capable of, Sherlock looked like a praying mantis thinking about anything other than a higher being. He had an old-school upright style, his hands extended in a gangly, controlled weave. They were moving around a little, no contact but playing the footwork game. Tracking each other's lead feet, trying to isolate the centreline, miming punches as openings showed up. Pillow feinted a sidestep to the right and tried to circle out, and, for the first time in five rounds, Sherlock managed to cut him off, beating him to the spot and miming a sweeping left hook that might just have landed.

Pillow bounced almost two feet in the air and clapped his hands. 'See, man, you got some moves on you. You know a lot, but you're too rich to ever have defence.' Pillow skipped over a few steps, then effortlessly slip-pivoted through every quadrant of the ropes criss-crossing the air.

'I'm not wealthy.'

'Yeah, sure, but you've got money in your genes, get it?'

'No.'

'Whatever your bank account looks like, you've got gold bullion in your bone marrow, playboy. Fighting's been a rich man's sport and poor man's sport. Started as a rich man's sport. Nobles would sword fight each other for honour and glory and all that shit, right? In Japan, France, whatever. There are, were, and will be exactly zero peasant fencers. You feel me?'

'I accept the premise.'

'And every noble kind of fighting, there's no defence. It's all about how to land your shit and be honourable enough to absorb what comes back with a constipated, stoical kind of look on your face. Because nobody's gotta make money. Then, your martial art becomes a sport people do for cash, and it goes to the poor people. They take it over and make a living with it. So, the defence comes in. The further you get from the nobles, the better the defence gets, because you can't be trading full-blast shots for the fuckin' Queen's honour when you're fighting for your rent money. It's always been the poor people who figure out how to hit without getting hit back. Because they need to. And I can be rich and you can be broke, but your genes, Sherlock, the fabric of your soul, will never be poor. You can be broke, but you can get un-broke. You can't ever get un-poor.'

Holmes rubbed his giant jaw with two narrow fingers. 'While I trust your pugilistic wisdom, dear Pillow, I fail to see the logic of this assertion.'

Pillow slipped two ropes and sidled up next to Sherlock. 'I'm not saying rich kids can't fight. There's pussies in the ghetto and country-club Charleses who can knock your ass spark out. No doubt about it. Those rich kids never think they're getting knocked out, though. Right? They know it can happen, but they never quite think it'll happen to them, specifically. So' – Pillow bounced into his stance, and Sherlock followed suit – 'I did my slip and slide out.' He slowly repeated his exit, and Sherlock cut him off like last time. 'Finally, right? You been chasing me all night, and you never caught up, and finally you sniffed it out and you got me.' Pillow raised his eyebrows and Sherlock moved in again. 'And your blood has so much of the stock market in it that you don't stop to wonder how it finally worked. You're not asking *how did I catch him this time?* You just know you did because good things come to those with parents with money.' As Sherlock's left hook slowly drifted in, Pillow reverse-shoulder-rolled it. 'And I am poor. So, I know most of the time when you finally get what you were waiting for' – Pillow crawled his uppercut until the tips of his knuckles rested on Sherlock's jaw – 'you're just getting whatever they wanted to give you in the first place.'

16.

Kim was working with her amateurs by the time Pillow got to the gym. He knew better than to try her without putting in some sweat equity first, so he ran through his warm-ups, shadow-boxed, and did some bag work before he finally went to talk to her.

By then she was sitting on a bench, idly playing with one of her braids. As he walked up, she looked at Pillow the same way people look at a puddle of someone else's puke at someotherbody else's house party. Pillow raised his hands, presurrendering. 'Can I sit down?'

She flipped the braid over her shoulder. 'Can you sit on your ass? Fuckin' gee golickers, I'd say sitting on your ass is starting to seem like a specialty for you.'

Pillow flopped onto the bench, and because he didn't know what to do with his hands he clapped and held them. 'I got sick, what can I do?'

'Sick. Sure, whatever, man.'

'I don't know what to tell you, Kim, all right? I'm getting older, I have to listen to my body and do … '

'Oh, would you shut the fuck up, Pillow, seriously. We were already listening to your body. Remember? Remember how this should have been a twelve-week camp and we said no, wait, let's listen to your old-ass, weak-ass body and do an eight-week camp. Eight-week camp but intense. We said that, right?'

Pillow wiped some sweat from above his eyes, and after he hadn't said anything for long enough she slapped him across the back of the head.

'We said it.'

'We said eight weeks, full intensity, no bullshit. And now it's three weeks into that already too short camp, and you're still fucking off on me. It's over, Pillow. I love your dumb ass, but I can't do this.'

'I'm here right now.'

'I'm talking to you but are you here? Are you here to fuckin' train? Not just spar, do your bullshit footwork drills. I mean real work, with me. Doing what the fuck I tell you at the intensity I tell you to do it. Are you here for that? Because if you're not going to save your own ass, save mine. Remember? You go out there looking out of shape, what does that do to me, Pillow? You know how this game is. You slipping looks like me slipping. I need you to look professional. At a minimum. And I don't know if it can happen, you keep on like this.'

Pillow stayed quiet for a bit, trying to think about what Kim was saying, but really thinking more about how much of talking is just people who both already know things saying those things at each other. Thinking about how much people talk. 'I can't promise I'll be good, like, in my heart. But I want to beat this kid and I can, and I don't want to fuck with your money, so I won't. For real. Right now, five-week camp, we can do it. And next time, it's the real one. We do it together. Me and you all the way.

Kim wobbled her head around. 'Tell you what, I'll pray on it. The next one, we'll see how it goes. Meantime, though, let's get you back on with some shit you're familiar with.'

'Familiar how?'

'Familiar like you is with your living room wall, sunshine. Shark tank.' She smiled. 'Unless, what? You're not rested enough? Because a man takes days off, he's already ready, right? So, you ready enough to rest, you get that rest, I can call the boys over. Unless you got something to say about it.'

'Line 'em up.'

Gyms the world over have shark tanks, and they all work a bit differently. Some gyms have shark tanks where everyone is a shark. So, you start with two in the ring, whoever wins the round stays, loser leaves, and a fresh person comes in. The point is that you fight until you lose or until you're so tired that you lose.

Kim's gym wasn't big on teamwork. Her version of the shark tank was to have one guy in the ring going ten rounds with fresh partners rotating in. The one guy lasts the ten or quits. For a fighter of Pillow's level, at this point in the camp, it should be a difficult but very doable exercise. Also, if the exercise were for real happening and not happening as a punishment for endangering her career, Kim would have put a couple of easy rounds in there, guys who wouldn't trouble him. Instead, she had the ten best fighters in the gym lined up.

This little lesson Kim had planned was about the difference between being in shape and being in condition. Pillow was always in shape. Being in shape is what you get to by running, doing your ab work, hitting pads, touch sparring. Stuff Pillow did all the time. Stuff it just makes sense to do all the time when you're a man who was a boy they put in Spec Ed for emotional problems.

Being in condition means you're in shape, and your muscles have been hardened to take a beating from a grown man who was born and bred to beat people. Being in condition means you have enough shape to spare that you can walk out in front of thousands of people, take whatever beating comes your way, and still reflexively pull off moves that most people aren't coordinated enough to do once, preplanned, with plenty of practice. A couple of weeks of shooting liquid coke with Sherlock Holmes, a couple more days before the doping kicked in, and Pillow was sure he was in decent shape and really very far from decent condition.

He needed Kim in his corner. And, after everything, Pillow was a boxer not just on his taxes but in his heart. He'd avoid all the beatings he didn't need to take, but when he had one coming, he'd stand there and catch the whole thing, eyes open, on his own skinny legs.

The first two rounds went well. Pillow came in fresh, up on his toes. Knowing he was in for ten rounds of work, he didn't make much of an effort to win the first two. Mostly, he feinted and ran, circling the ring and making the sparring partners chase him. Kim had started him out with two bigger guys, a 168-pounder and a light heavyweight, probably hoping they'd lean on him and tire him out early. Pillow was too slick for that.

Feeling good, Pillow bounced back to his corner and took some water. It was hard to hear over the noise of the gym and through the headgear, but he didn't need to hear to know that Kim was promising to give the ten hundred-dollar bills she'd just pulled out of her fanny pack to whoever could drop him. There is very little in a boxing gym more dangerous than a sparring partner who's been shown a few bills.

The next two boxers were smaller and faster, and while neither of them was able to hurt Pillow, they did manage to make him work. Pillow had to sit down and fight off the ropes, spinning his man and smothering on the inside, mauling and grabbing. Kim swapped the order and brought in one of Pillow's primary sparring partners, an up-and-comer named Kassim, who hopped the top rope and screamed 'G-Ball!' before sprinting his entire round, throwing about 120 punches. Kassim had enthusiasm but not the skill to match, and Pillow picked off the punches with his gloves and elbows, sitting down on some hooks to the body hoping to slow the kid down. Kassim just kept at it, windmilling his punches in like he was providing clean, renewable power to a small Nordic fishing village.

The next round, Kim sent an out-of-shape super middleweight who manhandled and laid all over Pillow. Clinching and pawing with his punches, not doing shit really, but draining the last of the energy from Pillow's legs just in time for Kim to let a twenty-year-old Mexican welterweight in there to press him for three straight minutes.

When you're out of shape you get winded. You run out of breath in your lungs. When you're out of condition you run out of oxygen in your blood. You're not out of breath, breath is out of you. Pillow's knees were weak as he went to the corner. He had three rounds left.

By now, Pillow didn't even try to move. Kim rang the bell, and he stayed in his corner, slumped against the ropes, waving the fresh sparring partner in. The kid charged forward, right into Pillow's clinch, which allowed Pillow to kill a few seconds before he punched the kid square in the dick and bought himself a bit more time while the kid walked it off.

The most over-discussed concept in the history of boxing is the rope-a-dope. Ali vs. Foreman, the Rumble in the Jungle. Ali, brilliantly, goes to the ropes, tires out Foreman, and then comes from behind to vanquish the giant. It happened one time. Nine hundred ninety-nine times out of a thousand, the guy lying on the ropes taking a beating is doing it because it's the only thing in the world he can do right then. So, when Pillow went immediately back to the corner and absorbed about forty punches on the ropes, he wasn't doing the rope-a-dope. He was just doing what he could. When the round was over, Pillow didn't go back to his corner, he turned around, rooted to the spot, and hung both hands over the top rope. Pillow had never drowned before, but he was pretty sure this was what being 40 percent drowned felt like.

He'd gone the last minute of the previous round without throwing a punch, so he had a bit of gas back by the time the next round started. Playing possum, Pillow drifted off the ropes as the bell rang, and he got lucky, the guy had five hundred-dollar bills taped over each eye and rushed forward recklessly, missing a windmill right hand. Pillow slipped it and put everything he had into a counter left to the liver, sending the sparring partner cringing to the canvas. Pillow had just spent the last real substance in his body, but he would never spend all his style. He pointed an exhausted arm to Kassim and screamed 'G-Ball!' at the top of his spent lungs.

All other activity in the gym had stopped during the shark tank, and a crowd had formed around the ring. As soon as the kid hit the ground, the whole place went crazy. The shark tank broke down as everyone rushed the ring, and Pillow let himself relax into a mess of bodies who held him up and pounded on his shoulders.

Boxing fans think that what they see is what counts. That everything else is just practice for the fight. What fighters know is that when you're actually taking the punches, every single thing counts. The first fight you have isn't a fight for a belt, or a purse, or a win on your record; it's a fight to survive. It's that time when you really don't know anything, when every day you're riding the subway home with a headache, your gym bag stinking, your back sticking to the seat, and one day they throw you to the wolves. They stick you in there with a good fighter, bigger than you, more experienced, better trained. They want to see what you have, what you can take. Before you can do anything, before the amateur tournaments, before the fights, you have to pass the test. Those aren't fight nights, they're random afternoons at the end of practice. They happen every single day, and nobody sees them, except everybody there. If you've ended up becoming a fighter, that means you survived. You passed. Every fighter can tell you about that day, the gym fight where they didn't bitch out. What happens in the gym isn't practice for the thing, it's the thing.

And so it didn't matter if Pillow lost this fight and ten more after it. No matter what he did in public, everybody who was there would know, and if somebody said Pillow's name to them, they'd whistle, and they'd say that guy was the real shit. They'd tell the story about the time he sucked his heart off the ground through his asshole and body-shot KO'd a light heavyweight.

Pillow felt as good as a person can feel when they're too tired to feel whether or not they're peeing. He'd waded through the crowd, stripped off his gear, and was now lying flat on his back in the corner of the gym where the battle ropes were tied up. There was big flat board over the window, with a hinged cut-out you could open to see the sun as a treat. Kim sat down on one of the ripped punching bags on the ground, slowly disembowelling itself into a loose pile of sand. Measuring the distance casually and perfectly, she lofted a protein bar to land in the middle of Pillow's chest.

'Eat up. Dead motherfuckers don't make weight.'

With great effort, Pillow lifted his right side just far enough to tip the bar over onto the ground. 'I'm eating. Trust me, I'm eating.'

Kim used the toe of her shoe to push the bar closer to Pillow's blindly fumbling hand. 'I'm not talking about pretzels and fuckin' giraffe food, man. Protein.'

Pillow nodded and sat up, started unwrapping the bar.

Kim gummed the end of one of her braids and let it drop. 'Pillow.' She broke into a small, shrugging laugh. 'I don't know if you're the luckiest or the unluckiest fucking guy in the world. Every time you're about to learn a lesson, you pull something out.'

Pillow started working his way through a bite. His jaw was very tired. 'I learned. Message received, trust me. I am not in shape.'

Kim shrugged, no laugh this time. 'I don't nag nobody but you, Pillow. Nobody in my whole life would call me a nag. A cunt, sure. Lots of people. Crazy person, psycho, serial domestic abuser, all kinds of shit. A nag, never. Nobody but you because you know what?'

Pillow's jaw was working too hard to say *what*, but it was rhetorical anyway, so he just focused on chewing and keeping all the liquids still in his body in his body.

'Because I've trained with everybody and I train everybody. I train heavyweights, 270-pound monsters, and I never felt like I couldn't kick their ass if I really had to. I would knock out every single motherfucker in this gym. That's a thing I know.'

'That's a thing is known.'

Kim pointed at him between his eyes. 'Except you. You got little bitch hands, you're out of shape, you're no bigger than me. But I know that some-fuckin'-how, I couldn't ever kick your ass for real. For good. That's a respect I pay you, Pillow, when I deal with you. So, you do shit that I would kick anyone else out of this gym for. Instead I nag you. I'm not going to threaten you anymore because we both know it's a lie. I'm going to roll with you, and I'm going to ask you to do right by yourself. And you do what you want, okay?'

Pillow didn't say anything and chewed one bite of his protein bar for over a minute. Then he swallowed, slid over to Kim, kneeled at her feet, and tenderly kissed her hand. 'There was a while where everybody around me was somebody I was paying or somebody hoping to get paid soon. And I didn't have a real friend in this world. You're my friend, Kim. I'm going to pull this off. It's me and you, ride or die.'

She patted his hand. 'Ride or die. Right? That's what you said. Ride or die. Let me tell you, it ain't ever ride *or* die. It's both. You ride and then a while later you die. So, I want you to go home and think about how often you get to choose, and what you get to choose. And then, if you want to, come in and train tomorrow. And the day after that and the day after that until you fight.'

Pillow stood, and when he got standing he closed his eyes, a little bit because he was dizzy and mostly because of his feelings.

After he left the gym, Pillow kept his appointment at the Childhood Cancers Ward and played *Fight Night Champions* with a dying twelve-year-old boy for an hour and a half. He gave the boy a pair of signed gloves and a T-shirt.

17.

Swimming is a great way to train for boxing not because they're similar sports, but because of exactly how and in exactly what ways they're different. Abstractly, swimmers race each other, but what they're really racing is the clock. There's no relativity: if you're a great swimmer you get great times. Boxing is always only relative. You don't race the clock, you work it. If you're a smart boxer, you figure out the best ways to eat that clock, the best ways to let it tick down without doing a thing. Swimmers refine their technique, but their effort never changes. Always, they're just going harder. Any energy they save is put into the next stroke. If you're a pure boxer, you learn what happens while all the things that never happen are somehow busy never happening. You learn how to clinch, how to smother. How to make the other guy take three steps when all you did was take a fraction of one and pivot.

As a young fighter, Pillow had boxed on his toes every minute of every round. Moving all the time. Now, he'd stand still until the other guy made him move. Instead of firing a flashy combo and leaping out of range, he'd throw a counter shot to the body and jab out, take two small steps clear. In his younger days, he tried to win every second of the fight, and now he tried to win every second he needed. Pillow was too old and too smart and too sad and too tired to want to win all the time, every second. Now, he spoiled every fight he was in joyfully and with a commitment to showing how cool it could be to squeak by. Not racing the clock, not racing yourself, not racing a thing. Just taking things as they come.

Kim was starting to get through to him that for this fight he had to be a swimmer. Three minutes a round, Pillow was going to be sprinting. Pounding the body, bringing it back up to the head, moving, feinting, punching, as long as his hands allowed. The last place he wanted to be was the gym, but the second last was dead tired in the fourth of twelve rounds against a guy who looked like every *Men's Health* cover squeezed into one shiny, photoshopped set of abs.

So, he was swimming. Pillow's swim training was systematic in the way hospitals were systematic before anyone knew what germs were. He'd look at the giant, melting clock overhanging the lip of his pool, wait for it to strike a new minute, then swim the length full blast, with a terrible, desperate, high-energy stroke, then he'd check the clock again, gulp air until it hit the next minute, then swim back as fast as he could. He'd do that until every limb on his body was tingling-moving-to-numb.

Sherlock's body responded to cardio by becoming first just some bones and then a little bit of dust, so he waited on the pool deck reading a scientific paper about how quickly wax falls off a windowsill.

Pillow hit the lip and used the energy he had left to wave, and Sherlock hustled over and helped haul him out. Pillow stayed flat on the deck of the pool for a while, his abdomen heaving up and down.

Sherlock checked his pocket watch. 'Have you the strength for the sauna?'

Pillow gulped more air, raised his thumb.

'Excellent, I shall fetch my costume.'

Pillow's sauna was old-school banya-inspired. It had a giant wood-fired oven with a grate that looked like it had been recovered from a tsarist mass grave. He kept a few soaked birch leaves to whip himself and increase the heat. He'd sprung for the coned sauna hats. The two men took their seats.

'So, Pillow, another day off from your trainer?'

'At the end of the day, aren't we all our own trainer?'

Sherlock laughed and pointed his weather-vane nose to the domed ceiling. 'It is so freeing when deduction is no longer required.'

Pillow took in a lungful of hot eucalyptus and coughed it back out. 'No, I'm taking a second to get me ready for the big push. For real. Last few weeks of this camp, I'm going all in. You know what I mean?'

'You're asking after the meldonium?'

'I am asking' – Pillow horked deeply into his throat – 'after the meldonium.'

'I have a regime planned for you. I should point out, however, that I cannot in good conscience recommend to you the remedies that science demands unless you are committed. These recipes are intended only for those in serious training.'

'It's serious.'

'And the materials for your hands?

'And the hands.'

Pillow was more used to feeling incredibly dizzy than most people, so he just waited it out.

Sherlock stretched his legs to their full length. 'Pillow, I have a confession for you. Or, as I know better, I shall reframe: No confession is for the other, it is only for the other to hear.'

'Shoot your shot.'

'I have spent the bulk of my life accomplishing feats and garnering acclaim. I have done so secure in the knowledge that acclaim is not the natural outgrowth of esteem but rather a confused aggression the mediocre inflict upon the talented. I have spent the bulk of my meagre life trying as vainly as I may to focus the obsessions of my mind on those things that may do some small good, to flatter the judgements of myself and anyone who chanced to look.' Sherlock sipped from a glass of water then dumped the rest over his head. 'If it would have worked, I'd have happily played with a ball and string, all day, every day. If a ball and string could quiet my mind. If the perfect chemical synthesis could. If a life full of gardens could. They cannot. And so, I sit, a retired detective and secret master chemist in a sauna with a great boxer, who is my friend and who is in danger, and I am thinking only of crime. Of that which may be solved. The mystery of whatever will not happen to Violet Hunter and whatever could have happened with Arsène Lupin.'

Pillow's headrush was over. He'd caught the last half of what Sherlock was saying, enough to get the idea. 'Have you thought about a girlfriend?'

Holmes slapped one side of his Everest widow's peak. 'Data! Data! Data! I can't make bricks without clay. It is always waiting that defeats me.'

Pillow patted Sherlock's wet leg then flicked sweat off his hand. 'You know why that is?'

'I beg you to tell me. For an answer would resolve the torture of my existence.'

'You're white-knuckling and battling. Fighting all by yourself and all the time and waiting's not doing a thing. Waiting's not even waiting. It's just being a word and some shit a word talks about.'

Sherlock took a deep breath, then wracked a smoker's cough so hard they had to leave the sauna. Pillow helped his friend gut through it and stared dreamily at the tiles, thinking about un-sad ways for sloth best friends to eventually die.

18.

As Pillow gratefully ate his way through a massive quantity of joyless green lentil mush, he watched the man who'd convinced him to go vegan eat two eggs and five slices of bacon for lunch. Pillow had been edgy and thought the drive out to Painlevé's place might be calming. He liked to look at the ocean as he ate. Painlevé was excited about a new buyer for Rigoberto the shark but didn't have anything committed in writing. Mostly, Painlevé had been enthusing about a new camera lens and Pillow had been complaining about how hungry he still was as he ate.

Painlevé polished off an extra graphic slice of the thick-cut bacon and dabbed the corner of his mouth daintily. 'Pillow, I've been thinking about this making-weight trifle of yours, and I have not come to a solution.'

'We can probably just skip whatever you have to say then.'

Painlevé waved him off. 'No, no, no. I think this might help your mindset on these matters. Here. See, it is natural to mistake our physical world for one that is scalable.' A hideous stork landed on the railing beside Painlevé's arm, squawked loudly, then walked on its impossible, fractured-looking legs off the balcony. 'A wonderful object lesson in just what I'd like to talk about, the impossibility of weight and angles.'

'Let's hurry this up a little. I'm due at the gym.'

Painlevé nodded gamely and continued. 'It's easy enough when we imagine the world as flat little pictures. Take a picture of a man, keep its angles in a constant relation to one another, and you can blow that picture up to ten times the size and have it maintain ten times the surface area. But take that same man and make him into a man-shaped cup. And, right next to this man we'll put another man-shaped cup in the exact same proportions but half the size. Then, we fill up the cups with two taps of beer flowing at the exact same rate. And we'll see that the larger man-shaped cup does not take twice as long to fill, but rather eight times as long. Where did we lose the time? Was it time we lost or space we gained? You've lost thousands of pounds in your life, Pillow. Where did they go?'

Pillow had thought about this. 'Didn't go anywhere. It was all water weight, so it evaporated and rained on somebody eventually.'

Painlevé smiled, then lurched forward trying to catch a pig-burp with his hand.

The animal-rights pitch Painlevé had used on Pillow at this exact table not so long ago had been intended to convince Pillow to give up his exotic pets and find more humane homes for them, and by the end of it Pillow had committed to giving up his pets and beginning a lifetime of veganism.

Painlevé's point was that what's wrong isn't so much the killing of animals, since killing is the natural condition of animals. From the top of the food chain to the bottom, one is always being eaten by someone else. Even humans are being constantly feasted on by microbes and worms and insects, just not often in a way they notice or are bothered by. What's wrong is mastering animals. Asserting authority over things that haven't, shouldn't, and wouldn't even know what authority is. It had made a righteous kind of sense to Pillow, who felt that it's only okay to dish out something you're willing to take. Pillow would never agree to being bred to be eaten or kept in somebody's house forever and never, ever meet anyone else of his own species. So, how could he do it to someone else? Even if that someone else was as stupid and objectively annoying to be around as a chicken.

Painlevé wiped some grease off his plate with a slice of bread. 'Say you took a man who weighed 154 pounds, as you aspire to. And we increased his size ten-fold. Because of the pesky matter of volume, he would now weigh not 1,540 pounds, but rather 154,000 pounds. But his tibias would only be ten times larger, and he'd collapse into a pile of bloody bone dust.' He leaned back in his chair and looked out at the sea, presumably done.

'And how does any of the shit you just said relate to any one of: getting rid of my animals, making weight, winning my fight? Anything that matters to me at all?'

'Physics would tell you that by the principle of mechanical similarity, a grown man would move half as quickly as his son, who was half his size. And we know that isn't so. Somewhere in all that math, which has to do with speed and weight and time, there's some little, uncountable thing that matters more. Which is rhythm. And maybe Julio Solis is bigger and faster than you. But when we're talking about living things, time and speed and weight matter less than timing and rhythm and spirit. So, you worry about your training, I'll worry about who is going to care of your pets, and we can both sit here quietly on this deck for a little while listening to the ocean. We'll do our sitting secure in the knowledge that nobody who cares about speed and power and force knows what the fuck they're talking about in matters of the heart. Which just happen to be all the matters that matter under this tiny, sexless sun of ours.'

19.

Being filmed doesn't take a tiny part of your soul, it just shows you what you look like without one. Seeing yourself on television is a lot like a kale smoothie seeing the shit you took after drinking it.

Right on time, a van pulled up. A middle-aged man with clear plastic glasses and a matching clipboard got out of the driver's side and a sexlessly thin woman with features 15 percent too big got out the passenger side. She waved about 25 percent too enthusiastically and smiled, looking like she had about 150 percent too many teeth. Pillow smiled back. He had about 90 percent as many teeth as you're supposed to.

The thin woman did some enthusiasm: 'Pillow! Great to see you again!'

'It sure is.' Pillow tilted his head to try to get a deeper look into her mouth. Did she have a second row of teeth, like a shark?

Glasses-Clipboard stuck a hand at Pillow and said a name the boxer felt no need or ability to remember. Pillow reached around the outstretched hand and tapped its knuckles with his fist. 'So, you guys are here all day, yeah?'

Glasses-Clipboard knew the score, moved right into it. 'Yes. So, regular training stuff today. We coordinate on your schedule and next rest day we come back for B-roll shots and the sit-down interview.'

'Cool, cool, cool. You need Kim?'

'It's taken care of. We talked to her.'

'All right, man, sounds good. I'll go get warmed up and then you can just start shooting. I really don't give a shit what you film of the workouts, but no sparring.'

'Sounds good.'

Too Many Teeth jostled him playfully by the elbow. 'And we can't convince you to show us some rounds?'

'I'm shy. Sometimes, I'm so shy I don't even want to exist.'

Glasses-Clipboard had already moved on. Too Many Teeth was smiling into empty space.

Pillow was somehow still professionally successful, so until now he'd always had more positive motivation than spite. Pillow supposed this was the turning point to Palookaville. That fork in the road where your hitchhiking thumb turns into a middle finger. He hoped this would be a quick detour, that he'd win and have more to look forward to next time. More money and a better idea of what to do with it. For now, he had to work with what he had, which was a powerful resentment of a seemingly sweet, definitely simple man named Julio Solis, the reigning champ, giving him a shot at the belt.

Julio Solis's lower abdominals looked like a newborn mountain range. His obliques looked like an ocean trench where they find fish who look like rocks and don't have eyes. Julio Solis's face looked like the feeling you get when someone explains something really complicated and you just wait and say *wow* when they're done.

So, as Pillow cranked out jump-squats and clapping push-ups, and as he ran pads with Kim, as he looked as smooth, sharp, and motivated as he had all camp, he wasn't thinking about himself. He wasn't thinking about how he looked, or the joy he took in his craft, or all the fun he'd have after he was done putting in the work. The only things running through Pillow's mind were the things Julio Solis would miss out on after he lost. The only feelings belonged to Julio Solis, and they were feelings he planned to hurt very badly. Going sixteen straight minutes on the speed bag, Pillow wasn't even thinking about the punches he'd land; he was thinking about the sweet, confused look on Julio Solis's face after he swung his fist at a head and hit the empty air it left behind.

To the untrained eye, there was not much to dislike about Solis. He was a quiet, committed young man who thanked his mother and his preacher about three quarters of the time he opened his mouth. He'd never said a bad word about Pillow or any of his opponents. By any reasonable standard, he was a kind, hard-working young man who loved his family. By Pillow's, he was an okie-dokie, yes-sir-no-sir-sorry-sir hump trying to prove that lacking the imagination to do anything but what you're told is the same as having a talent.

At the press conference announcing the fight, Solis had slumped over the podium and said thank you to the press, that he was honoured and grateful to be there. Right then Pillow knew he hated the kid. Honoured to be there. Grateful. Honoured to be in the presence of some sleazy fight promoters and twelve shitty reporters? The kid was either a liar and a suck-up or too stupid to draw breath, and Pillow didn't need to know which it was to know he owed him a beating.

Then there was the fact that nobody expected Pillow to win. Solis was a huge junior middleweight, who would likely finish his career two weight classes higher and still look big. Pillow was the smallest, lightest puncher at 154 pounds. More than the size difference, though, the odds were influenced by how terrible Pillow had looked in his last big fight. Getting stopped in ten rounds by a guy everybody was calling the Serbian Manny Pacquaio. Halfway through the second round, Pillow had already eaten about twenty lead lefts, and he'd realized suddenly and completely that the kid's hands and feet were quicker than his. Pillow had changed plans and tried to fight on the inside and very quickly realized that the Serbian Manny Pacquaio had faster hands and feet *and* stronger legs than him. Halfway through the sixth round, Pillow had run out of ideas, and from there had been, for the first time in his life, a journeyman. A guy who gets paid to take a beating.

He'd been outclassed, lost every round. 'Pillow Fist' Pete's welterweight run was over; it had been fun while it lasted, but it wasn't lasting any longer. Pillow agreed, but while everyone who couldn't see his bank statements and who hadn't seen how well he'd always done sparring bigger guys in the gym said that meant retirement, Pillow had announced that he was done as a welterweight because he was just starting as a junior middleweight.

Promoters and managers think things through, on paper. They game it out and they read the numbers and then they follow them. Pillow watched tape. Julio Solis was a thunderous puncher and a decent technical fighter, but he was also pampered. He'd won his title early, and now his people were protecting him and holding the belt hostage. His last two fights had been weak mandatories, small-time fighters for small-time cheques. Solis's handlers were waiting for someone else to get a couple belts, and then they'd gamble it all and try to unify. Pillow watched all the fights, and he saw the pattern of it, the way they'd worked it. And he'd seen it all fall into place at once. Pillow had a name and he couldn't punch a lick. He'd be a perfect stay-busy fight for Solis. The kid's handlers would see washed-up 'Pillow' Pete Wilson in the top fifteen, and they'd be coming to him with an offer. He wouldn't even have to chase it. So, Pillow had worked the rankings, won clear decisions over four club fighters, paid a medium-sized bribe, and gotten a short-money fight for the belt, with every advantage going to the champ.

Pillow had seen what he'd needed from Solis. He'd seen little cringes from body shots. He'd seen confused head shakes and tiny arguments in the corner of fights that weren't going perfectly. He'd seen a whole lot of hard, brittle strength. Pillow knew that he could trick this kid, but that wasn't enough. Pillow was slick enough to trick anyone in a fight, for a while. What Pillow knew about this kid was that tricking him would break him.

As he got in to spar, Pillow closed his eyes and imagined Julio Solis saying 'grateful,' and Pillow shouted to the camera crew.

'Fuck what I said. Let him see the sparring. Let him get a preview. Let him see these old legs about to run his ass off a cliff.'

The crew filmed the twelve best rounds of sparring Pillow had done all camp. To the man himself, it would look how a loose shit looks to a kale smoothie, but to everyone else it looked like an old, smart fighter doing the only thing he knew how to do, the only way he knew how to do it.

20.

As a treat, Pillow drove to a fancy part of town and stepped into a small metal tube where the temperature was −145 degrees Celsius. He stepped out of the tube and about three quarters of the blood in the whole city rushed into his muscles at the same time. He felt a little dizzy. Pillow rubbed the textured rubber gloves they give you over his torso, enjoying the scrape over his raw, active nerves. He took the gloves off and stood still for a while, feeling blood and the wet air it carried move around the wet inside of his body.

The boxer realized that there wasn't a door anywhere in the room, and he didn't remember how he'd come in. The only exact second you give a door your attention is right when you need it, and you need it only until the second you touch it. Probably there was a door on the outside, and it looked like a normal door, and he'd just used that. He sat on a bench that was also a perfectly clean white rectangle and put on his clothes, and he stayed there another few seconds, feeling his skin touch the inside of his clothes until they were familiar enough to feel like nothing at all.

Extreme cold on his skin and in his muscles was a thing Pillow had convinced his brain and body was good rather than painful and terrifying, but he hadn't convinced his soul. He knew that you can freeze a glass of water, turn it into ice, then melt it, and it'll be just as much water again. He knew that in his brain, but he still couldn't quite convince himself it was true, that some tiny thing wasn't lost in the transition. So, he supposed he'd been in a rush to get out of the cryo-tube, otherwise he would have noticed the marble statue at the edge of the room earlier.

Pillow was a statue guy. He owned one and he'd shopped for several. He respected all artists, and sculptors especially. To look at a rock and see a jacked discus dude with a tiny dick is real talent. He wandered over to the statue and gave it a thorough once-over. It was a solid piece, travertine rather than marble, which was cheaper but worked in this case, gave the carving a little texture. A young, armless woman with short, curly hair in an ankle-length robe. Bit of a cop-out to punt on the legs, in Pillow's opinion, but the face was well done, more detailed than the human face it was based on in that way only a real sculptor can hit. The stubs of her shoulders were smooth, so you could tell the statue was made without arms instead of having had them fall off over the centuries.

It's hard to become a statue guy without hiring a professional statue guy to teach you the basics. And Pillow's professional statue judger had told him that looking ain't shit in the statue game. It's all about that touch. Your fingers on the stone and the movement you can feel in a rock so heavy it takes a crane to budge. To be worth buying, a statue has to have some movement in it, some give or resistance to the kiss of your fingertips.

The boxer closed his eyes and brought his open, scarred hand to rest gently on the statue's face. He opened his eyes and saw that all the veins in his arm were bulging out from the skin like anchor ropes straining against the side of a boat, and he stared at the path of his blood, which seemed somehow to be going to the statue rather than his heart. Even though he knew cryotherapy just makes you super vascular afterwards, he let himself rest there, eyes trained down the gentle gun barrel of his arm, imagining that his blood was pumping into the statue. Not waking it up but filling the eyes enough to say that they were closed by choice, and he felt the statue's eyelids plump up and settle down under his fingertips as he stared, unblinking, at a rock that hadn't moved since a forklift dropped it in that exact spot.

When he was fifteen years old, Pillow had bought himself a fly swatter and then every day for a year he had come home from school and slapped himself in the forehead with it for an hour straight. The point was to train out the flinch reflex, to learn how to blink by choice. He wasn't sure how long he stayed in the cryo room, but it must have been awhile, because by the time the attendant came to get him his face was freely leaking water that was only there because of how much air had been touching his eyes. On the way out, he'd offered to pay $25,000 for the statue and given the owner $3,000 in cash as a down payment.

Wandering out of Blood of the Poet Health and Human Optimization, Pillow should have been feeling elevated. Healed, prepared, and pampered. But, leaving the door and looking out into an industrial complex that was a few bushes and a small fountain and twenty-five glass doors, Pillow didn't feel optimized, he felt another way.

His body beat up, out of condition and over-trained already, the right thing to do was go home, drink calming tea, stretch, and go to sleep. One more time Pillow didn't do the best thing, he only did what he could. He took off down the road, running the twelve miles he needed to get home. Once he was there, he weighed himself, saw that he was two beautiful pounds down, and then stared at his body in the mirror, flexing. He depilated his shoulders, then took a shower so hot he couldn't expose his genitals to the stream.

The boxer towelled, walked downstairs nude, nodded uninterestedly at his roommate in the salon, and microwaved a large container of wild rice and chickpeas and ate it, staring vacantly at the marble table, so tired he couldn't think, only hope, and so tired that the only thing he could hope for was a little bit of sleep.

Part II

Pillow Covers

I.

'A thing so complex as Africa can't really be said to have a middle, so I hope you'll forgive some scientific and spiritual imprecision, Mister-Doctor Painlevé.' Gwynn Apollinaire spun her flintlock pistol by a trigger guard the shape of a mermaid with no tail, bringing the barrel to rest on Painlevé's forehead. You could tell it was a mermaid just from the hair and that impossible angle a mermaid's breasts always sit at.

Painlevé bumped the barrel back with his forehead. 'I'm neither a mister nor a doctor, and certainly no one to be offering forgiveness.'

Gwynn smiled and spun the pistol to rest under her own chin. 'In the middle of Africa there's a lake filled with mosquitoes. No people, no animals for miles that are also days sinking in sand. Nothing to bite. And the only thing these mosquitoes know is how to die in a day.'

Pillow rotated his ankle a few degrees to the left. It made a thunk as low and blunt as the world's largest raven flying into the world's cleanest window. 'For real?'

Painlevé reached over and petted Pillow's ankle like it was a dog about to be put down for arthritis. 'It is for real, although not an entirely accurate framing. See, as a matter of fact and conscience, the mosquitoes don't fill the lake, they people it.'

Apollinaire made a fist on top of her head then made the fist brains explode. 'I'll permit you to correct my facts but never my fancy, Painlevé.' The barrel flipped back to Painlevé's forehead, and she cocked the flint back. 'You'd do well to remember it.'

If he had been a careful person who planned things, Pillow could probably have ended his career-threatening association with Gwynn Apollinaire's clearly insane and reckless and only very loosely organized crime syndicate several years prior. On the other hand, if he had been a careful person who planned things, Pillow probably would have been lucky to end up a night-shift manager at a chain of twenty-four-hour treadmill gyms. So, it was hard to regret being who he was and how he'd done things.

Gwynn's office was four white walls and a desk that was more like an overgrown music stand. On her desk, a fur-covered coffee cup and saucer with a fur-covered spoon sticking out. Apollinaire leaned back in her chair, pointing the flintlock at the ceiling and aimlessly stirring the furry empty cup with the furry empty spoon. 'Now, Pillow, don't fall asleep on me here, but we've got a long-term business offer for you, Jean and I.' She dropped the spoon. 'The scam, which will begin in a few months' time, is that our boy Painlevé has gotten himself access to a near-infinite supply of high-quality anabolic steroids through his connection at the zoo.'

'Like, people steroids?'

Painlevé became a man you never see talking over a screen showing a bunch of gorillas just being themselves. 'In captivity, gorillas are treated with the exact same drugs and for many of the same diseases as human beings. Most gorillas you meet at the zoo will be on some manner of cholesterol medicine, for instance.' When you're a man who is a voice talking about gorillas it feels right to go on uninterrupted for as long as you need to make your point about gorilla health. 'Another major issue is early onset andropause. Absent any threats, the little fellas, by which I of course mean the gorillas' already minuscule dick and balls, just wither away. To keep their lives worth living, the zoo pumps them full of exogenous testosterone. Which they order by the barrel-ful and have shockingly shoddy inventory control over.'

Pillow hoped it was fake fur on the coffee cup but knew better than to ask. 'Cool scam, but I'm not looking to get titties. I need speed, diuretics, and endurance drugs, not shred-my-joints and break-my-dick pills. Sherlock's got me covered.'

'As your sponsor, I agree. Anabolics would be a terrible look for you, ruin that svelte,' Apollinaire ran her hands the length of Pillow's imagined thigh and shivered graphically. 'Just every morsel as lean and spiralled as a hemp rope holding tight the yearning of a sail. As erotic as a young aunt's cunt glimpsed from a moderate distance.' She sighed abhorrently. 'While you must maintain your current regime, I was hoping to get you into distribution. You have direct connections to a massive number of men who desperately need discrete, untraceable steroids, and packaged with some of Sherlock's tried-and-true methods of obscuring these substances on drug tests, I think we can all see the potential profit.'

Pillow nodded and flexed his jaw, which thunked sickeningly and gave him an immediate headache. 'Yeah, I'll mull that over. Can't be talking business for real this close to a fight, but that sounds good to me.' He wiggled the bottom plate of his jaw and something clicked into some place. 'It's sad about the gorillas though. Like, maybe they're better off fighting and getting killed by a lion. I just don't know anymore.'

Painlevé patted Pillow's hand. 'If you knew before, you're better off now.'

Gwynn levelled the pistol at Painlevé's head and pulled the trigger, and some empty gunpowder did what gunpowder does when there isn't anything around to be pushed by fire.

2.

As often happens with roommates, Sherlock's mental health seemed to be on a pendulum with Pillow's. The more Pillow crushed out training sessions and actually did all his physio exercises, the more days Sherlock strung together sitting in a weirdly erect posture chain-smoking bowls of shag tobacco and throwing aside the newspaper after trying to read it for a few seconds. Doing exactly nothing but waiting for Violet Hunter to call and angrily trashing newspapers that said nothing about Arsène Lupin.

Pillow had a profound and subtle respect for the power of moods. The solution to any short-, long-, or no-term problem is to approach it with a good mood and an open, calm mind. This was a thing Pillow knew alongside another truth: that you can't generate a good mood where there isn't one. So, Pillow would give Sherlock his time, but that time would be limited. When you're living rent free in a boxer's mansion and you're still allowed to keep a quarter stake of your doping lab with no upfront investment, that boxer should not be doing his own laundry and vacuuming your tobacco droppings.

It had been an amount of time that Pillow almost certainly could have calculated given several minutes, a calendar, and access to his own Wikipedia page since he'd cut his entourage down to Sherlock and the exotic animals. In whatever amount of time that had been, Pillow had mostly adjusted to the solitude. He was able to see its positives, the freedom he had, the absence of day-to-day stress. But he did miss having people around, laughing at his jokes, complimenting his muscle definition, doing his chores. The real thing he had to remind himself any time he felt the entourage itch, was the looseness, the calm, the air in his lungs he gained from the simple absence of people fucking stealing from him. All he had to do was remember how much it hurts your feelings when people you love look at you and only see things they want.

The entourage, which had gotten three dozen deep in its heyday, was down to Sherlock and Rigoberto. Pillow still wished that it could be one sloth bigger.

Until recently, Pillow would have said that animals were his favourite things in the world. He loved them more than cars or houses or clothes. Animals were his thing. And so the idea that they were not things at all had set off a slow-blooming sadness in him. He'd always known that animals were alive, that they had thoughts and feelings and everything. But Pillow had been blinded to the real ethical stakes of animals' happiness in the same way a lot of people are.

From the time you're a child, you're taught to think of animals as functional objects. Things that you eat every single day with a special bonus option of being adorable and really connecting with you on an emotional level when they're not being food. So, it had been easy and fun to buy the coolest animals he could think of and keep them in his house. It had felt so very much better than keeping twenty-four humans around twenty-four hours a day just in case he started thinking about how much easier it had been to remember appointments and names when he was younger. The more time he'd spent with Jersey Joe, and the more time he'd allowed himself to be by himself, the more he'd started to pick up on the sloth's melancholy. The way Jersey Joe would nibble at a banana and leave the end because it was just too much effort. The way he'd tap on the walls with his sloped, clipped-off nail beds.

He'd talked about the whole thing for hours with Painlevé and Genevieve, and they'd been chill about it, but had made it clear how wrong it was to keep his pets, and how very much pain even the dumbest animal feels when they're not in the right place.

That was certain, but what Pillow was still thinking about was all the uncertainties, all the questions that smart people look at you like you're dumb for asking but can't answer. Like, which animals are smart enough to have feelings? If you put a leopard in a room with leopard-print wallpaper, where would that leopard think she was?

One thing Pillow couldn't get past was that most of them don't have sex for pleasure. Something happens in their brains and their bodies power up to do it. To go through the whole thing, to make a baby and then care weirdly deeply about it, all with no real decision being made, without liking any part of the whole thing. Just some hidden trigger somewhere deep in their shallow brains.

And this is where captivity came into it. Obviously, it was wrong. But how wrong exactly nobody could tell him. For one thing, almost every wild animal lives longer in captivity. Mostly that's because they're not getting randomly eaten and, longer term, the stress of worrying about getting randomly eaten has been removed from their lives. Pillow wondered, does that make them happy? Are there animals dumb enough that the absence of danger adds up to joy? Are people those animals too?

For a fighter, things that a lot of people call their entire rich and productive lives are called distractions. Family, friends, love, sex, the stock market, questions about what it means to be alive: these are all things boxers are told are in their way. Things to be dealt with later, after it's over. After the camp, after the fight, after the next camp and the next fight. After all the next fights are done, you can think about how you want to be in the world and what you want to be like. But if you've got a fight scheduled, thinking like that will take your mind off what's important: the always task of being your best and using that to beat someone else. To a boxer, life is a distraction.

Pillow heard the doorbell ring. He didn't move from his chair. He waited a beat, turned to look at Sherlock, who was, right that second, a used to-go coffee cup that had been left on someone's desk so long they've started putting used tissues in it. The doorbell rang again. On the way past Holmes, Pillow flicked him hard behind the ear.

'When company leaves, we're having a talk.'

Holmes's eyes darted up for a second and then dropped listlessly back to the ground.

'Some shit's a-foot, Sherlock.'

Painlevé was at the door, looking like he usually did, like there was some kind of bright horizon behind whoever he happened to be talking to. He popped his hand up for a wave and held it there. 'Pillow, allow me to introduce Mr. Wilk. He's from the shark rescue habitat we've been talking about.'

The guy Painlevé was introducing looked like he'd walked off the screen of a silent French movie. Like when movies were just a train ride. Pillow hated handshakes, so he shot the guy a wink and made a *gotcha* sound with his mouth. Mr. Wilk the shark lover did a little bow.

'An honour to meet you. Really, an honour.'

'Sure, sure. You wanna see the shark?'

Wilk grinned. 'Absolutely. You wouldn't care to validate my credentials?'

Pillow waved him off, transitioning into an elaborate over-the-shoulder point to the shark tank. 'I'm sure you're all good, my man.' As Wilk started toward the back, Pillow stopped him with a soft press to the middle of the chest. It felt like getting handsy with a loose breeze. 'I'm not a paperwork guy. But if you want to see my shark you've got to look me in my eye and tell me Rigoberto's going to have a happy life with you.'

Wilk looked at Pillow's throat for a beat, then set his posture and locked eyes. 'I can't promise that a captive apex predator will be happy. I can promise a humane living situation for a relatively low price.'

Pillow moved his hand up to Wilk's shoulder, patting him solidly with the heel of his hand. 'Fair enough, fair enough. Let's meet your new friend.' Painlevé and Wilk moved for the back door, and Pillow dipped back, peeked into the living room, and raised his hands at Sherlock. The detective stayed perfectly still, staring at the ground.

As always, Painlevé was locked on the shark, staring into those black, empty eyes. Wilk was angled a bit oddly and seemed to be more interested in the tank. He gestured past the shark, which was biting empty water and shaking his head back and forth, pretending he was shaking all the blood out of a surfer. 'And he's been eating dead meat mostly, correct?'

'Yeah, I grab him a fish at the pet store when I can but … '

'You can't keep up with the volume.'

'Yup. You know sharks, I guess.'

Wilk grabbed Pillow by the elbow and shook it. 'It's perfect. Our sanctuary takes sharks without properly developed hunting instincts and gets them acclimated in a controlled environment. The goal is to release them to the wild within their lifetime.' Wilk leaned in. 'We're at the cutting edge of behavioural modification in this species.'

Pillow did not like Wilk. He shook his elbow free and slid the back door open. 'How many get released?'

'About 20 percent. It sounds low but it is a beautiful, beautiful number. I love this number. Nonetheless, one must always pray for the lost … ' Wilk closed his eyes and dipped his head to his chest. Pillow caught Painlevé's eye and rolled both of his. Painlevé nodded and made a keep-it-chill gesture. Wilk moved closer to the tank and looked it up and down again, sizing up Rigoberto. 'He's about three years old?'

'Yep.'

'Perfect. I have seen all I need to see.'

'That's it?'

'No, no, I'm afraid that's far from it. There's the paperwork, but I trust … '

Painlevé finally piped up. 'I'll take care of the paperwork, and, Pillow, I'll call you with the date once we're set up. There's really no hurry since you're in camp.'

The shark man took one look back at Rigoberto. 'After the official details have been finalized, the date is up to you, Mr. Pillow.'

The reason Pillow had been scammed so many times in his life was not that he was too trusting. Pillow deeply distrusted and was intensely turned off by literally every person with whom he did business. Anyone trying to sell anything. The problem was that he did, eventually, have to do business, and so Pillow's undifferentiated distrust had often led him to miss the differences between scam artists and honest people who just sell medical insurance. Wilk had a slick, businessy vibe, but his offer seemed legit. Probably that's just how you have to be to keep a shark sanctuary running.

'Don't put a *Mister* on a nickname.'

'I apologize.' Wilk had closed the distance. He held his hand out, not taking no for an answer on the shake. It was a perfect hand. Thin, strong fingers, just the right number of veins. His nails were buffed and clipped, with a tasteful, clear microlayer of polish. The shark man's gorgeous right hand made Pillow immediately self-conscious of how mangled and hacked up and full of his own hip bone his was. He gave a limp, quick shake. Wilk grinned like they'd signed a trade accord enslaving the global south.

Painlevé had picked up on Pillow's extremely obvious distaste for and misplaced aggression toward the animal rights activist who was solving a major problem for him. He jumped in. 'So, Mr. Wilk, we can go back to my office if you like.'

The shark man nodded, looking at Pillow as he spoke. 'Let's do it, Jean.' He did a musical-theatre pause. 'Say, who was that man in your living room? I swear I'd seen him … '

'I'd guess you didn't. He doesn't get out much.'

Wilk popped his head back a little, and Pillow watched as he formed and then smartly withheld a follow-up question. 'Ah, it's of no consequence. I will be so glad to welcome Rigoberto into our family.'

That part, Pillow liked. He was tired of talking, so he let Pain-levé see the guy out. Pillow stayed in front of the tank awhile, watching Rigoberto move slowly to tag up on the edges of his tank then listlessly rolling to another. Over and over, just tapping the glass and moving on to the next piece of glass. Pillow hoped that Rigoberto's brain was a little smaller than it seemed to be. That it was just the right size to mistake safety for joy.

3.

Pillow was standing in the middle of the terracotta section of his driveway with a white pillow sitting in the middle of a bright pink circle. He'd done it at least a bit as a joke that cost $35,000, but he couldn't remember which bit had been the joke, exactly. In any case, Pillow had a really ugly and expensive driveway now.

'Sherlock! Get out here.' The boxer was feeling a little keyed up and happy to be out in the sun, so he really didn't feel like going all the way down to Sherlock's dank bedroom to wake him up. He figured with the right weighting on the throw, he could reach the window with a tap that wouldn't break it, even if the only rock near him was a little big for the job. For the first time in several years, he regretted not having a coin on him. For the first time in several years, he realized it had been several years since he'd had a coin on him.

If shovels kiss the ground, the rock kissed the window. Pillow could hear the sheets moving around. A widow's peak floated into the framed nothingness of the window.

'If I may … '

'My window, my bad, my problem. Get out here.'

The widow's peak bobbed up and down and disappeared from view.

In the harsh light of the morning, Sherlock looked somehow dusty and waterlogged at the same time, like an old treasure map somebody left out in a misting rain. He must have really had a night, because he had his deerstalker pulled all the way down, trying to shade the black pits around his eyes.

Pillow patted him on the shoulder and thought for just a second about spiderwebs and how long and thin and weak a thing it's possible for an entire species to live on. 'Listen, we've both had our moments here. But Arsène Lupin is in jail and that teacher ain't calling. Or if she is, it's not the juice you're looking for.'

Holmes nodded. 'I had theorized similarly.'

'Right. So, we could try to deal with whatever problems you have or … ' Pillow spread his hands and gave his best local-car-wash-commercial smile. 'We can get you going on a mystery!'

Sherlock looked about as enthused as a fresh grape meeting a raisin. 'I appreciate your efforts, however I am loath to trawl for cases … '

Pillow stopped him. 'No, no. The case is right here, baby. Where my car isn't.'

'You mean … '

'I mean my car is gone. Somebody stole my car.'

Sherlock looked like he'd mainlined two IV bags of espresso. His eyes were already darting over the ground. 'Well, dear Pillow, that is not in evidence. We simply know that it is gone. The most beautiful and overlooked step in the solving of a crime is establishing whether one has occurred. To establish what, indeed, a crime may be, and only then to conclude by exploring the trivialities of who may have chanced to commit it.' Holmes stroked his chin and scanned his eyes all the way along the driveway without moving any other part of his body.

'Fuck, I told the car service I didn't need a ride today.'

'And when was the last time you saw the car?'

Pillow winced and tried to think about the feeling of driving. 'Uh, I don't know, maybe last week. It's super hard to keep track of days. I'm assuming you're going to want to grill me on when I … '

Holmes held up a finger. 'Indeed, but it can wait until I've completed a thorough examination of the scene. I have a feeling the answer to this one lies in the dirt. Also, you must go train.'

There was a long enough pause.

'Just say it, man.'

'I fear the becoming of what I am.'

'Just say it.'

Sherlock wrestled a full smile down to slight twitch of the very corner of his mouth. He stood to his full height and threw his head back, stuck a finger up in the air. 'The game is afoot!'

4.

Arriving at the gym, Pillow would have wished to see absolutely anyone but Vince Harris shuffling around. In his day, Vince had been a *motherfucker*, a huge lightweight with blazing hand speed and knockout power. Vince had about ten great years, another two good years, another one that was fine, and then eight that were an important notch or two below awful. It's a typical path in boxing: you make your name, and by the time you get the big fights for real money it's already too late.

In Vince's case, this meant that by the time he got his dream fights his hands were just a little slower, and he had a wide-awake grown man's problems. As a boxer, you're lucky to keep half of your own action. You pay out 10 percent for a trainer, 15 for your manager, another 10 for the promoter. You pay your sparring partners and the cutman, so whatever you see a boxer making, cut 40 percent right off the top, then know that the taxman's coming for half of what's left. And then, you might say that's still a lot of money. Half of 60 percent of millions is still a lot. But, in Vince's case, a lot became a little real quick, between a couple paternity suits and a divorce and an entire extended family with their hands in his pocket. By the time he lost his belts for the last time Vince was already cheque to cheque, needing a mid-six-figure payday to keep up with child support.

Vince was lurking beside the front door pretending to look in his gym bag. He pretended to notice Pillow walking up, pulled it off about as convincingly as an eight-year-old showing a magic trick. It took him a couple false starts before he got his trembling lips moving the way he wanted. 'He-he-he, hey Pillow, my man. Whazzup? Whatzzup with you, man?'

Pillow stuck his hand out and Vince seized it for a quick bro hug. 'Usual shit with me, Vince. I got a fight coming up.'

'You good? Your peoples are good?' Each word sucked and smashed down like an old juice box.

'All my people are good, Vince. Everyone's good.'

Vince kept taking tough fights because he needed the cash, fighting guys twenty pounds bigger and a decade younger than him. For a while, if you were a welterweight prospect who wanted to add some shine to your resume you fought Vince Harris. Every few fights, one of those prospects wouldn't be legit and Vince would knock the guy out. Coming off the win, a top guy would take a fight with Vince for an easy win with name value, and Vince would take another righteous beating for a semi-decent cheque. Start the whole process over.

And now, shambling around the front of the gym hoping for a handout, there wasn't any process to start over. There was just the one process that moves in only one direction. 'We fight, Pillow, when's that? Five years ago? Whooping you put on me, must have been one of the last ones.'

'About seven years ago, maybe eight.'

'Maybe eight, shit. I gotta get … ' He pointed a trembling finger at his gym bag. 'Get back in shape, why I come. You know, get in shape, see about, about, about some work. You need sparring partners? I don't look like too much no more, but I give you rounds, Pillow. One thing you can say, I give rounds.'

Even as he slowed all the way down, there was one natural attribute Vince never lost: his chin. Vince Harris could take a punch. In his prime, Vince had borderline Hall-of-Fame skills. To the very end, he had an All-Time-Great chin. Vince had had about seventy fights, lost twenty, and finished all of them on his feet. Now, sitting on a bench in front of a gym, stains on his sweatpants, dried spit at the edges of his mouth, Vince staying down wasn't a question. Vince was down, and when a fighter goes down for good there's no one there to count to ten. There's just you and the floor and a clock that never stops.

'I'm good on sparring, Vince.'

'Sure, sure. Yeah, I get it, you still big time, right? I tell you though, you put the word out for me, Pillow. You put the word out. I know the look, but, but, it ain't about what the look is, man. I'll give work, I'm ready. Born ready, maybe I take a fight, see. Show what I got, get a little work in again. Three weeks I'm ready.'

Vince hopped off the bench and started shadowboxing. And for the next few seconds Vince was himself again. The looseness went out of his body, the rhythmic bouncing and twitching he did to cover his shakes went away. Vince settled in, throwing tight, fast jabs and right hands, that great hook to the liver. He bounced on his toes, hit a shift into a left hook. But he stopped after that and settled back down on the bench, sucking wind. He started up with some nodding, noticed his lip quivering a bit. 'See, man, these hands they're … they're a gift. Gifts the real … When God gifts you, you … shit happens and all, but you keep it. You keep the gift, right? If it's really a gift, it don't ever go away.'

'Yeah, I see you. I see you, Vince.'

Their fight was the only time Pillow'd really wished he had power in his hands. Just a little. Vince had been his first step up against a big-name opponent. At this time, there were still plenty of top guys Vince could beat, but Pillow was too slick, too fast, too careful, the worst possible matchup.

There are so many ways to quit in a fight. There are the obvious ones: you can stay down instead of getting back up, you can quit in the corner, you can say *No mas*. But there are other little ones. You can keep touching a cut. You can start grunting when you get hit, let the ref step in. You can pull up short, stop putting your weight in your shots and let the guy you're fighting know that it's safe to carry you. You're not trying to win anymore, only go the distance. And this was a deal Pillow was always willing to take. He had brittle hands anyway, so if a guy was willing to give up the rounds, Pillow would carry him across the finish line every time. Vince never made any deal. He never let himself get carried. He was always there. Like a cat, he'd pounce the second you took a step backwards. If you clinched up with him, he'd be there, whacking you on the hips. Vince made you beat the shit out of him. So, that's what Pillow had done.

Vince rubbed his stubble for a bit, gave Pillow the bluff smile again. 'Say, it's ... I know I'm not giving the work, but ... if you got a little money.'

Pillow patted him on the back, put his gym bag down, and pulled out a $500 roll in twenties and tossed it. Vince dropped the roll, hung his head for a second, then picked it up, shaking the cash at Pillow. 'You good, Pillow. You good, man. Couple fights, maybe, just some work, I get it back to you.'

'Don't worry about it, Vince. I'm flush.'

Vince sniffed and picked up his gym bag. 'You flush, sure. You flush, but I'll ... I'll get it back to you. After I get my workout in, maybe see ... '

'Vince, Kim doesn't want you around anymore, remember? She'll be mad you're even where you're at now.'

Vince threw his hands loosely over his head, spit flying out as he shouted. 'Fuck that! Fuck that cunt, fuck her, man. That shit wasn't shit. Kick me out of a gym, I knock a motherfucker out, what? It's a fuckin' boxing gym. Motherfucker step to me, what I'm gonna do?'

'He was a kid though.'

'Fuck that noise, man! Fuck that. Everyone's a kid sometime. You step to a motherfucker like me you gonna get laid ... laid out.'

'He was twelve, Vince.'

'So what? I'm twelve years old getting dank pussy, fighting grown-ass men, all day. All day. Fuck that. That kid weren't no twelve years old, man. What're you talking about?'

Pillow brought his hands together in a prayer pose. 'Okay, Vince. Okay. You and me are good. But it's her gym, so I don't … You and me don't get a say, right?'

Vince nodded, looking at his shoes. 'Yeah, yeah, fuck that noise. It's … don't know why I come here. Plenty of spots for me to get work. But you need it you call me, I'm ready. Next camp, you call me, I give you a week free, pay this off. I give you that work.'

'Sure thing, Vince. Sounds good.'

The old boxer shuffled away without looking back. He reached the sidewalk and then looked around, as if surprised by the street. Vince stopped for a while, his head ticking around as he thought it through. Eventually, he picked a direction.

5.

Since the car had gone missing, Pillow had met Sherlock Holmes. The real guy, the detective. And, while it was nice to see Sherlock in his element, it also could not have been more annoying to live with him. For two days now, Sherlock hadn't been able to talk to Pillow without hammering him with questions about where he'd been, when he'd be there, who would know the answers to those questions better than Pillow did. It was relentless. And, to make it worse, he wouldn't even share any theories, he'd just nod or shake his head, go back to thinking silently.

A couple years back, Pillow had bought the full right-before-the-Feds-raid-as-they're-hosting-their-daughter's-baby-shower drug dealer security package. This was a 'troublesome piece of the puzzle' for Sherlock, and an ongoing concern for Pillow, so they were doing a walkaround of the grounds looking for possible points of entry.

Holmes was decked out in a deerstalker and a three-piece suit. Pillow was wearing underwear and diamond-studded blue blockers, air-drying his body.

'I must commend you, dear Pillow, on your decision to avoid the pernicious draw of the information age in not keeping the security camera footage from your home.'

Pillow did an impromptu hamstring stretch. 'No way I'm going to surveil my own self.'

'Indeed, the blunt certainty of video evidence poses as much a threat as the unreliability and illusory nature of that same evidence.' Holmes spun his walking stick in a circle, levelling it to point at the wall behind the pool. 'One final point of entry to inspect, and then we shall discuss our next steps.'

'You have a theory on this shit?'

'I have arrived at nine potential explanations, and, pending the completion of our facility inspection, three actions for us to perform. I am also in possession of one revelatory piece of evidence yet to have been graced by the warm grip of your cognition.'

Pillow was enjoying the feel of the air making chemical stuff happen on his skin. With Sherlock, you could wait out anything you didn't understand. He was going to keep talking. Holmes strode ahead, tapping the wall twice with his stick before dropping to a knee to examine something. Pillow tilted his head back and looked directly into the sun for a while and thought about what sunflowers think clouds are. Either seconds or minutes later, Holmes clapped him on the shoulder and pointed the walking stick at the back door. They joined arms and went inside.

It was colder in Pillow's house than it was outside, so he put on a pair of track pants he'd found draped over the kitchen island. Sherlock took a seat and lit his pipe. Pillow went to the freezer, grabbed a head of kale, three servings of sweetened BCAA supplement, and two bananas that had used to be separate whole shapes, then had been one liquid, and were now one oblong frozen shape. He bit the end of the shape and tried to swallow it with the minimum possible contact with his taste buds.

Holmes's eyebrows jogged three times as he puffed to get the pipe lit. 'Of one thing I may assure you, Pillow. I've a feeling that wheresoever it may be, your car is intact and has not been put to nefarious use.'

'Farious use only. I still need that car, man. It's … it's a lot of my net worth at this point.'

Holmes twiddled his thumbs. 'One supposes that doping laboratories do not factor into that particular calculation. As you should be aware, my industry has more than tripled … '

Pillow stopped paying attention to Sherlock bragging about his chemistry for the length of time it took to feel a chunk of sweetened kale with infinite corners squeeze itself down his throat. 'So, when do you think you're going to tell me these possibilities and things to do?'

Holmes crossed his legs archly at the knee. 'I still require more precise answers about your day-to-day movements.'

Pillow's thorax was cold. 'I don't remember, I wasn't keeping track. I used the car service or I didn't. I don't know. I don't not remember, I never fuckin' knew, okay? I got enough distractions, all right? Please just find my car.'

There was a long pause, during which Sherlock uncrossed his legs and leaned down, his hands over his kneecaps. Pillow apologized not by saying he was sorry but instead by closing one eye tightly and smiling with the whole rest of his face. Not sheepishly, but with sheep somewhere in mind. Sherlock smiled back with both eyes and most of his mouth and tipped the deerstalker at Pillow.

The bachelors retired to their respective rooms.

6.

To keep his training fresh, Pillow put on a suit with 2,000 cut perennials stapled loosely all around it and sprinted down an abandoned airplane tarmac until every petal of every flower was dying somewhere in the air or on the ground instead of on a suit on his body. He'd forgotten where he'd heard of this idea and why it was good for you. It was something about being a sad distant part of how the earth is supposed to work and feeling like that part for a little, while your strong, beautiful legs carry you until it's just you and a sack and all the air you can possibly grab with lungs. A lot goes into training for a professional fist fight. And most of it is pounding pavement or bags filled with sand you're pretending is a person or using a sledgehammer to hit but not hurt a giant tire. And sometimes, some of it is being a beautiful ball of flowers that sheds into a man.

Pillow was just starting to get into proper condition, and his body was starting to crave rather than resist the intense work-outs. His legs were just about there. He could go twelve rounds if he watched his pace. But he knew that wasn't enough. He needed his legs to be more than ready. He needed them to be full of what good dreams are made of, that thing just past an imagination. And he really hoped one more week was enough to get them there.

He turned back around and drank from his gallon jug and looked at the long trail of flower petals he'd left in his wake, and he watched the wind drop down in nervous sporadic gusts, trying to kiss them and coming in all teeth, blowing the petals away until finally they weren't gone, they were somewhere else. The gallon of water wasn't gone, it was every place in the infinite somewhere else of his body.

Several years ago, Pillow had started doing a bit where he always said *tummy* instead of *abs,* and in professional boxing that is what's known as an insanely interesting personality. The camera was the only thing in the room looking anyone in the eyes. Too Many Teeth was too used to green screens to pull off a one-on-one.

Pillow was the old, faded name fighting the hot young prospect. He knew what he was supposed to do here. Julio Solis had a body as hard as a rock and a personality as interesting as also a rock. Put a camera on this kid, he'd give you four platitudes and a smile. So, the promoters needed Pillow to sell the fight, give the whole affair a little life. Pillow had made many horrible professional choices in his life, as recently as a week prior, but he hadn't made any of them out of ignorance. Pillow knew this game. It was easy. Talk a little shit, maybe get in the kid's head a little.

Too Many Teeth smiled at nothing in particular. 'How are you feeling for this fight?'

Pillow winked at a window draped in a blackout curtain. 'How does a mongoose feel looking at a snake?'

'Good?'

'Well, okay then.' Pillow crossed his arms behind his head and leaned back in a way he'd practised in the mirror. His delts were popping this camp.

Too-Many-Teeth looked at just enough notes. 'Pillow, everybody knows you're a long-time pro. A lot of people have been wondering with the change in weight class whether or not you're still motivated for this fight … '

'Let me cut you off. Motivation's for when you're young, dumb, and full of cum. Motivation's what you use when you don't have what it takes to beat the man with your mind.' He pointed at his own temple, like a real asshole.

'Okay. But for curiosity's sake, are you motivated?'

Pillow nodded and, giving her a little credit, answered. 'This is a rough game, and I've been in it a long time. When you're young, everything good you do is good for you. Then you get old and the good shit you do is bad for you. I go for my run now and it's good for my wind, but it's fucking me up. Every step is grinding my ankle down. I train hard, wake up the next day – I don't feel stronger. I feel the same or I feel like shit or I feel the same and it's like shit. So, it gets hard. Right?' Too Many Teeth was actually looking at him now, and Pillow had always really liked it when a pretty woman felt sorry for him. 'But, once this whole thing got rolling, once I saw that I really have this shot … Listen, they fucked up and gave me a chance to show what I'm about. And now they get to see.'

'Is this fight personal for you?'

Pillow had warmed up to Too Many Teeth, but when something pissed him off it did it quick. 'That's a stupid question.'

Too Many Teeth looked like a dog she'd been rescuing from a ditch hopped out and bit her. 'Why?'

'Because everything is personal. Everybody wants to act like they're telling the truth. Saying it like it is. Giving it to you straight. And every single time, every single person is taking every single thing personally. So, yeah, this fight is personal. But it was also personal to me when I took a shit this morning. Doesn't have anything to do with what's left in the bowl, you feel me?'

'Was the shit as personal as this fight?'

'Nah, I've got my fibre going nice. Smooth machine right now. Catch me on a protein day we got something to talk about.'

The cameraman laughed. Too Many Teeth didn't, and the blackout curtain he'd looked in the eyes as he said it didn't either. Pillow guessed they were right.

And Pillow guessed that what he really wished was that whenever he did a beautiful thing it didn't pan out to a few dollars he spent instantly on not feeling like he wanted to die. That it didn't all come down to how many people would pay to watch the two loneliest men in the world try their very hardest to touch each other on television.

7.

Pillow had no way of knowing how long ago Sherlock had showed up at the gym, because when you're in the Palace and Kim calls 4 a.m., it's absurdly dangerous to pay attention to anything other than the hand weights flying through the air.

Kim had what some people called unorthodox training methods and the rest called some pretty weird and dark shit. As a fighter, she'd been known for her brutal conditioning regime: running in army boots, pushing a hand tractor, chopping wood, sleeping in a burlap sack. As a trainer, given time to think it through and make the plans herself, Kim's methods had not gotten any safer or more refined, just more particular.

Most of the Palace was a normal wooden jungle gym. At its highest about thirty feet, with most of the bars about half that distance up. It got weird only once you started looking at the sections, the carved Canada Goose framed by poles suspended by dried-out goat intestines. The rectangular cage with a strange, spike-lined squiggle of wood in the middle. The wooden thing that was half-woman half-bowling pin. The sanded-down tree trunk attached to a sheet of clean, white concrete. Strange as it may have been, the Palace was enjoyable to Pillow. Kim barked instructions at him and he scampered and climbed around. Sort of a free-form gymnastics workout. Things only got hairy when she called 4 a.m., which was just a mysterious way of saying you had to do all your climbing while she tried to bean you with curved three-pound metal hand weights that looked like caterpillars with giant eyes and no mouth.

If you're using a training technique that anyone in boxing says is a bit much, you can bet that anyone not in boxing would call it a felony assault. The Palace at 4 a.m. was definitely a stupid and dangerous training technique, especially a week or two out from a fight. But Pillow thought the hand-wringing was overblown. It's also dangerous to train for a fight by having people punch you. It's just a kind of dangerous that everyone's used to and involves fewer spikes and weird shapes.

Pillow made it through the Palace and dodged all the hand weights and was just warming up for his rounds on the mitts when he saw Sherlock sitting on the bench looking absently at the ceiling the way eight-year-olds do to show you they're being Not Impatient.

'You found my car?'

The detective hopped to his feet and briskly moved to join him. 'Sadly no. I am afraid the case of the missing car shall have to wait.'

Pillow finished his burpee, then leaned in close and spoke quietly. 'Dope problems?'

Sherlock held out a letter: 'Please meet me at the Black Swan Hotel tomorrow at lunchtime. Do come! It is Fucksville up here. – V. Hunter'

Pillow shook the letter, and Sherlock snatched it back gingerly with his forefinger and thumb to stop the sweat from soaking the rest of it.

'I like her.'

'She is, indeed, a forthright and charming woman.'

'You feeling any kind of way about it … ' Pillow tossed him a quick wink. 'Trouser-wise?'

Even though Pillow had specifically used a word he'd never heard before meeting him, Sherlock looked less than impressed. 'Other than that she has obliged me to iron a pair for the train, I feel no way about the young woman. Trouser-wise.'

Pillow laughed and began shadowboxing, circling around Holmes and lighting him up with flashy, pulled punches around his jaw and torso. 'That's what I fucking love about you, baby.'

Sherlock turned to intercept him, barely got a jab feint started. Pillow slipped, pivoted, and jabbed his way out.

'You never fuck. There's so much power in that. Back in your day, you just calling in the cops, the families, everyone and absolutely stunting, laying everything out how you figured it out, how dumb they are, and boom, here it is. That's busting a *nut*, right there.'

'So, to business … '

'I've got some rounds on the mitts, and then I'm on my own. We're going to meet the lady and solve the mystery, right?'

Sherlock pulled out his pocket watch. 'Our train is in two hours.'

Pillow shoeshined a half-dozen uppercuts into the empty air in front of his friend's chest. 'Perfect. Box motherfuckers' ears off by day, rescue maidens at night. Woo! That's life.'

Pillow knew better than just about anybody that it's always 4 a.m. in some palace somewhere, so he didn't even need to see the hand weight to know he should duck and let it sail on past.

8.

At the end of his mitt session, Pillow felt a familiar twang blossom deep in his trap, cut the round short, and went to stretch, cool down, and viciously dig into his shoulders with a fascia ball. The entire world had collapsed into a flat horizon where the only colours were occasional negative fractals floating by any time a trigger point referred into Pillow's brain when Kim came over and tapped him gently on the calf. He jolted, opening his eyes as a lightning bolt that was somehow also made of ice and somehow also on fire spasmed from his neck to the tip of his index finger.

'All good, Kim. All good, I'm on it.'

Kim twisted a braid, sucked some teeth. 'Get the rubdown later, too.'

'You ever known me to miss a massage?'

'Nah. I've known you to miss about a dozen.' They both laughed, and she whacked the spot she'd just gently touched on his calf. 'That's what they don't tell you about it before you coach. They say fighters will steal from you, they'll leave you for a big trainer, they'll get in bar fights, all that. It's all true and I don't care. But what they don't tell you is that all these fighters, all these male-ass fighters, are going to act like teen-girl cutters. You remember those bitches, show up with like a fuckin' anarchy sign cut on their thigh.'

'I'm guessing I spent a little less time in the girls' locker room than you did in high school.'

'I'm past guessing you spent way less time getting sad-girl pussy than I did in high school, big man. I'm knowing that shit for sure.'

Pillow eased his seizing back to rest against the wall. 'So, what's the bad news?'

Kim played with the small mound of scar tissue below her eye. 'I'll go good news first. You're looking better, for sure. Your wind is there now. Your weight's coming along. You got your legs under you finally.'

'But.'

'But you're not sharp like you should be, Pedro. You're just not. I'm not saying you're washed, but we needed the whole eight weeks. You gave me five. And it's not enough.'

Pillow let his head fall against the cold metal of the wall. He closed his eyes and listened to all the fists hitting all the bags and all the chains bouncing. The skipping ropes barely kissing the ground. The smell so strong and so bad your body and your brain knew enough to somehow keep it from your consciousness. Pillow opened his eyes again. 'So you think that. What do you want to do about it?'

She cast a quick glance back at the gym, tucked her shoulders up to her chin, shelling up. 'You need a few more weeks, maybe we talk to the doc, say you got a bone bruise. Push the date back.'

'If we push it, they're going to replace me.'

'Pillow, if that's how it is, that's how it is. This kid is bigger than you, younger, stronger. Sure, you're better, and sure, he's a basic bitch, but he can crack. I can't see you get hurt.'

Pillow tucked his hands into the warm damp cave system of his armpits. 'I'm looking that bad?'

'You're not looking bad at all. You're looking slick, you're looking smart, but you're not looking like the you I need to see. I don't see the snap. The fine edge. If they pull you, they pull you. I gotta do the looking out.'

The boxer tucked his thumb into his palm and squeezed it so hard it felt sure to break. He weighed his options and saw there wasn't much on the scale. He and Kim stayed a few inches apart, each of them looking not at the other's face but at all the parts that mattered, all the parts you move to punch. Everything that twists. Pillow grabbed her behind the head and pulled it into his shoulder.

'Thanks, Kim. Thank you.' They let each other go. 'I'm not saying I'll do what you want, but I did listen. I'll think about it. We train a couple more days, then we decide. How about it?'

'It's your show. I'd love to be wrong, but I'm not.'

Kim stuck her fist out for him to bump it. Pillow dipped forward and kissed the wide, smashed-flat top of her knuckle.

9.

Arriving at an expensively rustically appointed newly built old-timey inn, Pillow and Sherlock saw Violet Hunter on the patio leaning back her wicker chair, her head hanging down, a half-finished margarita sitting in front of her. Violet didn't notice either of them until Pillow sat down, at which point she launched forward like a jack-in-the-box too aggressive for children to play with.

'Boy! You guys are quick. Sorry that I've had half of the drinks it takes to make me tipsy, which is one margarita. Thank you guys so much for coming. For real.'

The waiter stopped by and Sherlock aggressively ignored him as Pillow ordered green salad no dressing without looking at the menu.

Sherlock didn't use a notebook so much as he turned the way his eyes and brain processed things into a notebook. 'I trust, then, that your safety and freedom are assured?'

'I can come and go when I'm not tutoring that hobgoblin piece of shit of a child. But the vibes are fucked. Extremely fucked vibes.'

'Details are the fuel of deduction, Ms. Hunter.'

Violet Hunter nodded back several times and steadied herself. 'When last we spoke we were all tracked in on the wife being a nutjob, and that has not been validated.'

'No shit?'

'Zero shit, sir. Zero. The wife is, in fact, so boring it's difficult to make eye contact with her. She is very young and beautiful but in a sort of undead way. Like, she is super pretty, but it's hard to imagine there's blood anywhere in her body or that she'd know how to use it if there was. Anyhow, I'm getting sidetracked by describing how boring she is. See, I have not talked to anyone normal – or at least flowy and conversational – since I talked to you guys.'

Pillow patted his heart. 'I love being normal.'

Violet Hunter, clearly not exaggerating the undersocialized thing, giggled and snorted very loudly, then rubbed the tip of her nose. 'Back to it: the missus is way younger than Rucastle. What I didn't realize is that the kids are by his first wife, who I'm presuming is dead, but nobody said. And the hot gossip I got is that the older daughter, who is not far off from Mrs. Rucastle's age, moved to Philly because she can't stand Mrs. Rucastle, which to me is like having a powerful hate for plain oatmeal. Anyhow, there is only the vile crotch-scum I have to look after.' She took a deep breath and sipped conservatively at her margarita. 'Listen, fellas, I am an early childhood educator. I love kids, and I know how fucked up and weird they can get and still be fine. This is the worst, most spoiled, most disgusting creature I've ever seen in my life, this fucking kid. Let's go through it.' She started counting off on her fingers. 'He's got a real Alfred E. Neuman thing happening, tiny little body, ginormous head, which is superficial, I know, but it does give a sinister air to a lot of his actions. This creature's whole existence, I swear to you, is just alternating between gleeful savagery and the lamest sad boy sulking imaginable. Like, with this kid, you're teaching the Marquis de Sade or Sylvia Plath on a rainy day, no in between. The only thing he likes is torturing anything weaker than himself: bugs, mice, whatever he can get his hands on. And I'm sure I don't need to tell you, Mr. Holmes, but developmentally speaking those kids never turn out right. Sorry. That was just a vent. He's not even the point of my story.'

Holmes patted her on the hand. 'I assure you that any detail you see fit to include has a welcome home in the sturdy cabin of my attention.' The detective flopped back into his chair and closed his eyes to listen. Moving against the backdrop of the cloudless sky, Pillow thought his nose looked like an old-timey battleship sailing home.

Violet Hunter cupped the sides of her eyes, as if putting horse blinders on. 'I'm going to try my best not to miss anything important or take six years telling the story. Quick and dirty summary, wife is boring, kid is a monster, and Mr. Rucastle is actually a pretty funny and charming dude. First couple days I'm taking care of this hellspawn kid and chilling in my room. The creature is gross and annoying to deal with, but they're good on my hours, it's a beautiful countryside. I'm going for walks. I'm finally finishing *The Brothers Karamazov*, and I'm starting to think I can tough it out for a year to make the rest of my money. And then the dress stuff starts.'

Pillow spoke with his mouth desperately full. 'This part sounds like it's going to be creepy.'

Violet Hunter pointed at him and then made the finger waver. 'Creepy, yes. But not in sex way, still no sex creepiness. Creepy like a quiet street.' She took a less conservative sip of her margarita and plowed on. 'A couple days in, he's getting me to try on the blue dress. Which is an expensive dress that stimulates zero feelings anywhere in my brain or body. A bit of a weird shade, but wearable. So, I'm in this dress now, they love it, praise, praise, praise and I eat dinner with them. Mr. Rucastle was really on one, had a lot of great jokes, good stuff. And Mrs. Rucastle is just sitting there like a stone. If stones also looked hollow somehow. I'm cracking up and she's sitting there silent. And we do it again a couple days later. One time, Rucastle gets me to read from a book to him, sort of arranges my chair in a vaguely uncomfortable way. But it's whatever. I'm thinking about my bank account. Then, I notice that there's been this guy, this French-looking dude, who keeps walking by and peering over at the house. I tell the Rucastles, and they are just sort of weird about it, and they end up insisting that I go to the window and wave him away, for vague reasons that don't make sense?' She paused to gather her breath.

'Please finish your story, Ms. Hunter. I find it a most investing one.'

'Next few days, creepy walk-by dude doesn't show up again. I say creepy, but even from a distance I can tell he's low-key hot in an aristocrat sort of way. Rucastles are being fine. The kid's still a fucking monster, but whatever. One night, I am bored as hell, so I start rearranging my room. And I find this little locked chest in the closet. I'm nosy … and no! I'm not nosy, they gave me the room. I take the chest out, pop it open, and there is a coil of my hair in it.' She instinctively reached for a spot above her shoulder where a beautiful, messy pile of her hair would have been. Pillow thought she still looked cute with the short hair. 'But! I donated my hair to charity. So, this can't be my hair. It looks just like it though. Same colour, same curl. It's maybe a tinch darker, but real close. Creepy close, if you will.'

Holmes rubbed the soft skin of his upper eyelid. 'I will, indeed.'

'So now, I'm in detective mode, right? I've got Sherlock Holmes backing me up, but I'm also ready to be Junior G-Man Violet for myself. See what I can see. I start snooping the grounds a little more, getting curious about the house. There's this whole wing that nobody uses, and one of the windows is boarded up. So, I ask Mr. Rucastle what's up with it. And he flips shit. He gets so mad at me. Says it isn't my business, and the window's boarded up because he's into darkroom photography.'

The entire salad was in Pillow's body now. He could have eaten another of the exact same meal and still been hungry. 'Red flag.'

'Uh, yeah, you're into darkroom photography? That's creep city. Also, I'm not seeing any photo albums around this place, y'know? So, Junior G-Man Violet is on the case now. And I've got to get into this boarded-up part of the house. Junior G-Man Violet sneaks Rucastle's keys while he's out and creeps on into the creep factory ... '

'Noooo.'

She slapped Pillow's arm lightly and tsk-tsked him. The whole margarita was gone now. 'Don't be a scaredy cat. I already did it and I'm fine. You have to fight creep with creep, dude, it's the only way. Anyhow, this part of the house is *sketchy*. It's just three upsettingly abandoned, dusty rooms, and one boarded-up one that is locked six ways from Sunday. Dead bolts, a chain, the whole deal. And then I hear steps in the room, and I see this little shadow pass by the crack of the door.'

Pillow twitched and reflexively balled his hands.

'You are right to be afraid now, boxerman, because this is when Junior G-Man Violet becomes normal-person-terrified Violet and runs the fuck away and sends for help.'

Holmes sunk down, digging his bony elbows into whatever flesh he had in his quads. There was a long pause. Violet looked a little embarrassed. She picked up her margarita glass and peeked to confirm it was totally empty.

Pillow used the toe of his shoe to massage Sherlock's calf. 'I think she's done, man.'

Violet nodded for a while before noticing that Sherlock's eyes were still closed. 'Um, yes. That's ... I can come and go, but I have to be back by four to look after the kid. The Rucastles are going to some neighbour's house for dinner.'

Holmes opened his eyes and patted her on the hand again. 'I can assure you, Ms. Hunter, that you have acted with more bravery and sense than even the most senior of G-Men I have had the dubious pleasure of meeting. I must, however, ask that you assist me once more this evening before abandoning these dangerous and malevolent people forever.'

Violet Hunter blushed. She looked like a very kind cartoon chameleon who'd just touched an autumn leaf. 'In for $60K of pennies, in for a pound. What's the plan?'

'Pillow and I will meet you at the house at seven o'clock. All we require is that you lock the child in his room. All relevant details shall be revealed at that time.'

'Let's do it!'

Pillow stuck his flat hand over the table and nodded at her meaningfully. 'Count us in, Violet.' Violet Hunter stuck her hand out overtop of his. At length, Sherlock joined them.

'One, two, three, go, Junior G-Men!'

The three of them threw their hands gleefully to the sky in unison. Pillow had always thought he didn't like teams, and he was starting to realize that he only didn't like team sports.

10.

While Violet went back to the house to put the kid away and see off the Rucastles, Pillow and Sherlock retired to a nearby clearing, where the boxer did a gruelling series of body-weight exercises and the detective sat on a nearby tree stump staring fixedly at the ground, chain-smoking.

Sherlock had somehow maplessly plotted a perfect route through the trees, and they emerged onto the edge of the property, the house nestled into a stand of trees so stark against the red, spreading bruise of the evening skyline that they looked poured out of metal. Violet Hunter was on the doorstep, smiling, looking like someone who would marry someone who'd never punched anyone else in the face. The two thin men glided to the doorstep. Pillow extended for a fist bump and Violet had her hands deep in her pockets, so she dipped forward and tapped his knuckles with her forehead. Sherlock looked like a dog who doesn't really know what a smile is somehow smiling.

Violet sunk her head close to her shoulders, as if it could shrink the sound of her voice. 'The creature is in his bedroom dreaming about burning an anthill or whatever he does in there. I locked it from the outside. Side note, every door in this house locks from both sides, which is as suspect as you can get with home fixtures. Anyhow' – she paused and straightened up – 'He's locked in, so I don't need to whisper. Fuck. Feels good but wrong to lock that kid up. Like, against my code as an educator, but with my code as ...'

'A Junior G-Man.'

'I was going to say person of taste, but also separately as a G-Man, yes. Thank you, Pillow. Come to think of it, I'm ditching the Junior.'

Sherlock nodded curtly. 'And well deserved at that. Now, tell me, Ms. Hunter, is there a back entrance?'

'Yes, it's a straight shot to the creep room.'

'Excellent, we shall follow closely behind. If you would.'

'Would and will! Let's roll, team.'

Violet Hunter led them around the back of the house, jingling a set of stolen keys over her head. They went through the back door and found themselves in front of a padlocked and creepy door at the end of a hallway creepy enough that no description could have captured it. Violet handed over the keys and Sherlock tried them all without success, but he did get one to work for the chain and padlock. Pillow pressed his ear to the door, which made all the sounds a padlocked door makes when the room behind it is silent.

Sherlock winced slightly and made his index finger and thumb into a music stand for his chin. 'I sincerely hope we are not too late. Pillow, may I borrow the force of your posterior chain?'

'You couldn't handle that force, baby, but I'll kick the door for you.'

Sherlock gave a ticking motion with his index finger and winked. Pillow kicked the door open on his third try. The room was empty except for a small basket of linen with a note sitting on top. It was written in script so flowery and hard to read as to seem actively socially aggressive, and as they were trying to parse it, they heard a gate clang shut. Violet ran to the window and looked out.

'Shitsticks! It's Mr. Rucastle.'

Sherlock tucked the note into one of the thousands of pockets in his hunting vest, and the three of them sprinted down the stairs. They emerged into the crisp, new-dark air of the night in time to see Rucastle's running form disappearing into the tree line, his car idling in the driveway. They went over to the car to check for Mrs. Rucastle, who was nowhere to be seen. Sherlock rested his hand on the engine block and seemed just about to launch into a detailed explanation of what had happened when they heard a low growl emerge from the emptiness of the night.

Pillow instinctively clasped his stomach. 'My tummy makes a lot of noises I don't know a lot about, but that wasn't me.'

Violet absently patted hers with one hand. 'Me neither. And I am acutely aware when my tummy is makes noises.'

Another growl rolled through the quiet air.

Violet's eyes bulged as if a child were trying to inflate her. 'He let the mastiff out. RUN!'

Sherlock grabbed Pillow by the arm and started leading him to the house. They made it about three steps before they saw the snarling, drooling beast of a mastiff standing under the lights of the front door, lit up like she was about to do a very angry, very hungry dramatic monologue.

The trio froze. Sherlock spoke out of the corner of his mouth. 'We shall pace slowly to our right. Am I correct in assuming the cage to our left is for this animal, Ms. Hunter?'

Violet nodded. Pillow had not noticed a cage.

They moved in a unison of small, shuffling steps, the top halves of their bodies still from side to side and heaving from front to back in time with their breath. The dog stayed where she was, an increasingly large and intimidating pile of drool accumulating at her feet. Pillow stiffly turned his head and finally saw the cage, which was very clearly a cage for a very dangerous animal. A while back he'd considered buying a tiger, so he recognized this model.

The mastiff started charging when they were only a couple feet away, and by some miracle of physics almost managed to catch them, skidding to a stop right as the door slammed in her snout. Pillow kept leaning against the door to hold it closed. Sherlock tapped him twice on the shoulder and pointed at the catch bolt with his eyes. Pillow let an impressively huge amount of air out of his lungs then collapsed to the ground.

Violet was also on the ground, and Pillow buttscooted over to join her. He jostled her lightly with his elbow. 'Didn't think to mention the mastiff, huh?'

She smacked herself in the forehead. 'Oh geez, yeah. I forgot that part when I was telling you guys. The giant scary dog was a whole thing that … you probably get now, having seen her. Sorry, boys, they marged me up. They hit me with the margarita.'

'They?'

'Me. It was me.'

The dog had pulled away from the fence to pace in a menacing way a few feet away, occasionally baring her giant shimmering teeth at nothing in particular.

Pillow patted Violet on top of the head. 'So, the dog has caged us.'

Sherlock smiled lightly. 'An irony I'm sure my recently minted animal ethicist friend appreciates.'

'I mean it's funny and fair enough, but I wouldn't say I appreciate it. How are we getting out of this cage? I've got a lot of important stuff to do tomorrow.'

Sherlock sighed, reached into his hunting coat and pulled out an outrageously long-barrelled revolver.

'Were you packing that the whole time? Like on the train?'

'Of course. I had a feeling we would meet with villainy.' Sherlock hefted the revolver skyward.

Pillow stood and used his index finger to pull the barrel to the ground. 'I got this.' He moved to the door and stood there a second. The mastiff had backed off about ten yards and started charging the cage. 'This is definitely going to violate my insurance.'

In a smooth motion the boxer shoved open the gate and stepped into the path of the rampaging demon hound. He judged the pooch's stride and speed and caught the exact moment she loaded her hind legs to launch. He step-pivoted, letting the dog sail past and into the blunt stillness of a cage that in a humane world would have been chain link and in this one was wrought steel. The tip of her smallest nail had traced a thin perfect line from Pillow's nose to the edge of the cheek, moving through his scar tissue like a hunting knife through a wedding veil.

The dog's legs splayed sickeningly out to each side as she tried to right herself, losing her balance and careening sidelong back to the ground. Just as she was pulling her final infinite mastiff leg under her, Pillow pounced, controlling her neck and one foreleg with his arms and sinking his legs to her hips to pin her back legs. The dog snarled and spasmed, snapping her teeth and licking wildly at her face as Pillow's blood spritzed over the two of them.

In the cage, Violet Hunter turned her back and sank slowly to her knees in that perfect way shock imitates calm. Sherlock cocked a leg back and fixed his hand to his hip, then extended his other arm to its full length, as if posing for a photo that would take several minutes to process. After a few seconds, he lowered the gun and used his bone-dry hand to pat the gentle flesh of Violet Hunter's shoulder.

Pillow rode out the dog's first burst of energy and then began to nuzzle his nose behind the mastiff's ear. The dog kept struggling, and Pillow kissed her through the blood. Finally, the animal stilled herself and lay flat and spent on her side. Pillow unhooked his legs. He laid down again and settled himself in as small and fetal a ball as he could into the dog's chest and belly. Pillow knew that to really gain someone's trust, sometimes you have to let them be the big spoon, even if you're taller than them or even if they're a mastiff. After some minutes, Pillow stood and the dog followed him, stepping into the cage as Sherlock and Violet stepped out. They closed the steel door, and the dog pressed her face into the bars and Pillow pressed his mangled hand back, letting her feel the scars with her tongue.

Dogs don't think or know a lot about surgical scars. They can learn a lot more than people can with their tongues.

II.

After Pillow'd called them in for a quick huddle that was really more of a three-way upper body hug, the investigators made their way to the kitchen to talk things over and also see if there were any leftovers or maybe just some loose fruit Pillow could have. The boxer treated his cut with some antiseptic and three butterfly stiches Sherlock had in one of the thousands of pockets in his hunting jacket.

Violet ran a hand through some hair she didn't have anymore. 'So, uh, what the fuck?'

Sherlock whipped the note out of his pocket and lofted it in the air, letting it float to a rest on the kitchen island. 'The answer to that, Ms. Hunter, is simply stated but deducible only by navigating the most byzantine of mental structures. We have been tricked.'

Pillow's face was settling down from the sting of the iodine. He took a bite of apple so hard he had to check his gold tooth with his tongue before he swallowed.

Violet was trying to read the note again. 'Is that an *L*? What a dickhead way to write an *L*.'

Sherlock paced a little distance away and began speaking as if there were about twelve more people in the room. 'Put more accurately and far less succinctly, I have been tricked and the two of you have been instrumentally incorporated into the framework of the ruse.'

Pillow dabbed his cut and winced, more from thinking about what Kim was going to say to/scream at him than the pain. 'Sherlock, just do the speech already.'

Violet's head popped up from the note. 'He really does that?'

'You're excited now, just wait. He did a parlour show last time he found my keys.'

'You will admit, dear Pillow, that it was a not insubstantial feat of lateral logic to locate car keys in the bottom of an ice cube tray.' Sherlock stopped pacing and nodded grimly. 'As to present matters: of the precise mechanics of this particular Rube Goldberg I remain uncertain, but of the creator, mechanism, and intended action of the machine I have a sturdy grip. If I may, Ms. Hunter, what is Mr. Rucastle's first name?'

Violet poked her chin. 'I guess I didn't say, hey? It got lost in the sea of weird shit. His first name is Arsène.'

The name did something close to ringing something close to a bell for Pillow. 'Arsène … Is he a fighter? Manager? Arsène … '

'And what, dear Pillow, was the name of the gentleman to whom you've entrusted the protection and care of your shark, our dear Rigoberto?'

'Uh, Wilk.'

Holmes pissily flicked the corner of his lapel. 'Wilk is Polish for wolf. And Arsène is the first name of Arsène Lupin, the supposedly captured archvillain of whom I have spoken to you for several hours on end.'

'To be fair to me, for a lot of that you were just describing newspaper stories, which is a powerfully boring thing to do.'

Violet patted Pillow on the shoulder and looked to Holmes sincerely. 'He's right. It's maybe the worst social interaction.'

Sherlock flipped his hunting jacket closed theatrically. 'Indeed, I shall take note of this point of sociality. But it does not change that this is the work of an unaccountable villain, Arsène Lupin. And, if I may allow myself to swim briefly through the swamp of speculation in which he seeks to drown me, Monsieur Lupin has learned the truth of my continued earthly existence and has sought to provoke me.'

Pillow snapped his fingers. 'The fuckin' car!'

'The car indeed, sweet Pillow. The car indeed. Lupin gained entrance to your home by staging a visit with your shark, thereby gaining knowledge of the layout, vital to a burglar of his craft, and stole your car from under my nose to taunt me. I fear, however, that the jest may not yet have hit its punchline.'

'I lose a Bentley because this Lupin guy wants to measure dicks with you?'

'So it would appear.'

Violet Hunter drummed her lips then banged the table and pointed at the detective. 'One: why and how did he find me and how did he know I'd find you? Two: what was the deal with the dress and hair? Three: how does this trick, like, do anything to you or matter at all?'

Holmes beamed the way a lot of people would at a child's first steps and the way he often did at a beaker turning a different colour.

Pillow patted Violet on the shoulder. 'That was G-Man as fuck. Congratulations.' She peeped a grin at him out the side of her mouth, then resumed a detectively expression.

Sherlock ticked points off his fingers. 'One, he found you, my dear, by investigating the practice of my dear friend Dr. Watson, whom I may guess is your family doctor?'

The boxer rested his hands on the kitchen counter and dipped as low into a shoulder stretch as he could. 'You knew she knew him, that's not even … '

'Indeed, dear Pillow, hardly a feat of insight on my part. However, close attention to discourse also allows me to further surmise that Ms. Hunter, whom I eavesdropped to hear describe herself as "into crime shit," is quite likely to be the only member of my dear friend Watson's patient list who could be cross referenced to a subscriber list from the Mysterious Book Shop in New York City, symbolized so neatly by the crossed dagger insignia on her key chain.'

Violet flinched toward her pocket, then stopped the hand and wagged it at Pillow. 'I'm not happy with this situation, and I see how this would get old if you lived with him, but this does kind of fucking rule. It's a good energy to be around.'

Holmes was in full flow. 'The answer to your second question as to the reason for the demands of cutting your hair and wearing a certain dress is simple not in a logical sense, but rather a fanciful one. These were simple lures which both preyed and depended on imagination. Of no significance other than piquing your curiosity and sending a determined, bored, and crime-fiction-addled young lady first to her doctor and then to me. Noise made with the express purpose of eliciting a signal.' He paused with three fingers suspended in the air, throwing Pillow a quick wink before tugging on his ring finger. 'As to the third question of how I am emotionally or practically impacted, the answer is but a word: *superbia*. Or, as the frightfully prosaic followers of modern tradition would know it: pride.'

Violet stood abruptly. 'That absolutely rocked, but I'm also upset, and regardless of all of that, I'm an early childhood educator first and a G-man second. I've left that kid locked in his room for … a bad amount of time.'

Sherlock took her hand gently in his. 'Sorry to say, Ms. Hunter, but you have been most ill-used in this entire set-up. You will find that the child is gone, and indeed was never forcibly confined at all. This entire household was composed of players in a drama for whom I was the intended audience.'

'Seriously.'

Sherlock nodded and dropped her hand, which she used to smack the countertop. 'That is Fucksville, man. That is Fuck City, USA.'

'You are, as always, apt in your analysis and precise in your framing of the situation, Ms. Hunter. For your part in this drama, you have been paid your $60,000, and if Mr. Lupin has remained the gentleman I have known him to be in the past, you should receive the remainder of your payment in due time.'

Pillow flicked his apple core at Sherlock's head. The detective snatched it out of the air and dumped it into the sink.

'So, she gets paid to be in on this little prank, and I get paid minus one entire fucking Bentley?'

'Knowing Lupin, I anticipate that upon returning to your residence we will find your car exactly where it is supposed to rest.'

Violet Hunter had stood to pace and was in the Sherlock Holmes's spot now. 'Okay, okay, so it's you two pricks playing mental grabass using peasants as toys. Sure, but how does trying to kill us with a mastiff fit into this gentleman bullshit?'

'An excellent question, Ms. Hunter, and one for which I've yet to construct a satisfactory answer, save that the only currency a gentlemen may truly play for is blood.'

Violet turned to Pillow and said, 'Do you believe this fucking bullshit?' with just a small tight sweep of her hand.

Pillow believed just about everything.

12.

Sherlock was back in thinking-so-hard-you're-worried-he's-going-to-spontaneously-combust mode on the train. So, Pillow and Violet decided to leave him and stand in the outdoor smoking area not smoking.

She ground an imaginary cigarette into the ground. 'I got to meet Sherlock Holmes, at least.'

'You also got to meet me. I'm famous too.'

Violet blew a noisy breath through gorgeous, curly bangs she didn't have anymore. 'Man, I know this was an adventure and all, but I'm leaving with sour grapes. I feel … instrumentalized.'

'Like a tuba?'

'Exactly. I'm a tuba. Sherlock's … like some other stringed instrument in another section, and this Arsène dude is the fat guy blowing air.'

'Who am I?'

Violet Hunter poked his fat, flat nose with her tiny, pointy finger. 'You're a timpani.'

Pillow looked through the dark at the shapes of trees rolling past in the wide open air. He wasn't thinking about crimes; he was thinking about all the other things that can happen when there's space and quiet.

Violet flicked away the imaginary cigarette she'd already stubbed out. 'Like, he gets to keep being Sherlock Motherfucking Holmes, and Arsène What'sHisNuts gets to keep being a gentleman thief, and I get to regrow my hair and never trust another living soul? The gentleman paid me, though, so I also have to feel weirdly lucky. And I do what? Buy into a tutoring business?'

'That sounds like a good idea.'

'It is a good idea, but I have to do it now as me. I'm not a Junior G-Man. I'm no kind of G-Man, I only got tricked into thinking I was for a day. I knew we were all just little tiny leaves being fuckin' blasted by dickheads with those loud leaf machines in the long run, right? I'm not an oligarch, so I'm an undergarch, I get it. But this made it a bit brainbreakingly literal for me, y'know? How am I supposed to trust life now?'

'Did you trust life before?'

Violet Hunter punched him in the arm hard enough to hurt just about anyone who didn't get punched a few hundred times a week for practice. She smiled, tossed what would have been hair but was now just her little head. 'I bet you think you're pretty smart.'

'I bet you're a losing gambler.' Pillow grinned. 'A tutoring company, hey? From what people told me when I was barely listening, businesses need early investors.' Pillow checked both his pockets, pulled a loose wad of bills from each. 'I got about $9,000 here. I'm investing it, like an angel invests.'

Violet looked low-key horrified. 'You carry $9,000?'

Pillow eyeballed the wads for a second. 'Maybe more like $8,500 now that I look more carefully.'

'You really just carry random knots of cash in your pockets?'

'Do you want $8,500ish?'

'Seriously?'

'You decide my slice of the pie. As long as I get a little of that tasty fruit filling, it's all good with me.'

'Are you sure?'

'Yep. I'm supposed to diversify.'

'You're really sure?'

Pillow flipped the biggest roll of bills at her, and it bounced off her hands before she caught it. 'The only thing I'm not sure about … ' He wiggled the next wad between his fingers then tossed it to her. ' … is whether that one is mostly hundos or mostly twenties.'

She puffed her bottom lip. 'And there's no strings attached?'

'We live in a stringless world, you and me.'

'I'm not used to depending on anyone.'

'Good, then you can stay that way with 8,500ish bucks in your romper.' He extended his closed fist, and she gently head-butted it while tucking the bills in her pocket.

'This is a jumpsuit, not a romper.'

'Well, I'm not exactly Sherlock Holmes, am I?'

She laughed a little, popped her eyebrows at him. 'You sure are not. Thank you, Pillow, for real. Thank you.'

Pillow nodded.

'How's the shark?'

Pillow smiled and almost regretted his gold tooth. But not quite. 'He's still swimming.'

'Because he's a shark.'

'And that's what sharks have to do not to die.'

They pulled into the station, and she slung her bag over her shoulder. Pillow waved at her with both hands. Violet moved toward the station, then she turned over one shoulder, in a real way, not trying to look cute, just trying to leave. 'Good luck, Pillow. I hope you win your fight.'

'Good luck, Violet Hunter. I hope you never need to win a thing.'

13.

For the length of the cab ride home, Sherlock stared out the window silently, sulking through the case. Pillow also stared out the window silently, not really thinking that cases are things particularly, but thinking hard about cuts, which are some of the realest things possible.

He knew abstractly that it was possible his career was over. If they pulled him from the fight, he'd never get another shot. But somehow Pillow felt certain that the fight was going to happen, that he could and would eat all the shit required to get this chance to do the one thing he still hoped he still thought mattered. To get into a small square ring with somebody for a while and just see.

A cut can't be argued with. It can be taken care of, and you can do a good or a bad job of doing that, but if the cut's too big or just in the wrong spot, that's it, the fight's off. This cut was bad, long, and deep, but it was in a good spot. A gash this size above his eye, he wouldn't be cleared to fight for months. Below the eye, they'd let him fight in a few weeks. So, Pillow didn't think through his cut, he just thought for a while about how it existed.

To this point, Pillow had conducted one of the least professional training camps imaginable. It had been a thing that even as he was doing it Pillow would have acknowledged was a disgrace to his profession. He was past his prime, fighting a future superstar, and he'd still gone through his whole disaster of a camp doing about a quarter of the bare minimum amount of work, completely confident he would win.

Just since the fight announcement Pillow had done dozens of things he wouldn't have been able to imagine on his own. Pillow had smoked angel dust with Sherlock Holmes. Pillow had spooned a sloth to sleep. Pillow had ridden a stationary bike twelve stationary miles in a tent where the air was as thin as if he was 6,000 feet into the sky. But losing this fight was beyond the realm of possibility. If he was being perfectly honest, he would admit that he had never considered it.

At the beginning he'd been confident that Julio Solis was not, in fact, the next best thing. Pillow had been sure he would expose the kid. And now, thinking about the couple millimetres of skin between his cut and the still intact eyeball just above it, he still thought he was right about Julio Solis, but he'd been wrong about Julio Solis being what mattered. If Pillow got the fight pushed, he'd have six weeks to make himself perfect. To do the thing he loved to do, and to use the gift of his body to do it.

Without feeling like any distance had been travelled or any time at all had passed, they arrived at Pillow's house. With little idea how much cab rides cost in general and no idea how much this one cost in particular, Pillow threw two hundred-dollar bills into the front seat of the taxi and a man who had as many toddlers in his home as Pillow had luxury watches he'd never worn thanked the boxer a few thousand times.

The front doors of Pillow's house were tall enough to make everything behind them seem fictional as they opened in front of you. And, even without the doors, Rigoberto, like any shark who lives without the context of living beings to catch and dismember with its face, had always had a bit of a ghostly and unreal feel to him. So, it took Sherlock and Pillow a minute to realize that someone had stolen Rigoberto.

A shark had used to be Pillow's living room wall, and now Pillow's living room wall was some water with glass in front of it. Sherlock nodded absently, seemingly unbothered that he had been wrong about the car being returned, and acting as if someone stealing an entire shark was some obvious thing that was always going to happen. Sherlock didn't even really bother to look for clues, somehow already knowing there wouldn't be any. Instead, he called Jean Painlevé.

As they waited and Sherlock paced a few miles, the boxer sat quietly on his giant peninsula of a couch, not thinking about anything at all, just feeling grateful for the only body he was ever going to have. No matter how easily it broke, Pillow felt, finally, that he could know his body for what it was. Not a sponge to be squeezed out or a rope to be unknotted, but a gift he could unwrap any time he wanted.

As he entered, Painlevé waved from under the doorway, which wasn't a magical gate to a magical forest grove, but should have been. And it wasn't until Sherlock stalked across his line of sight that Pillow remembered all the things someone had stolen from him to prove a point to his roommate.

'Hello, my friends,' said Painlevé. 'Sherlock, I assume you'd like to speak to me.'

Holmes's eyes had been replaced with a particularly unemotional and now dead guppy's eyes, but he still had enough politeness in his brain stem to take off the deerstalker as he walked into the house. 'I think, Mr. Painlevé, that the discussion you and I are to have is best framed as an interrogation. And I should like to have Pillow with us.'

Pillow stayed seated. He tilted his head to the side and thought about thinking about caring about things. 'I'm good, actually.'

'What?'

Pillow hopped up and put his arm around Sherlock's waist and leaned his forehead to rest on the crest of Sherlock's hairline. 'I trust you, buddy. You're a great detective. You should do your thing. But for me, the case was Violet Hunter walking away unsex-trafficked with a little cash in her pocket. And that happened, so my first and last case is solved. Me personally, I'm going to kick back and get ready to beg for my career tomorrow.' Pillow released the detective, spinning him into a handshake. 'Consider yourself hired. Now go get my shark and car back. Or, keep go getting those things back, I guess.'

For the first time since Violet's letter had arrived, Sherlock looked happy. Then, as if hit by a plate-glass window of serious-ness, he stiffened, grabbed Painlevé by the elbow, and led him into the kitchen to be interrogated. Then, for half an hour, the little Frenchman explained to the detective how he'd been tricked partly by a master criminal and mostly by his own guilt about loving animals so much he wanted to keep them and film them and keep the films of them forever.

Pillow heard it all without listening, and looked at what nothing looked like in a tank full of water that was also his living room wall. It looked like about half of his face, the good half, floating faintly on some impossibly thick glass, which had been some impossibly thin sand a very long time. Like any face in any glass, really.

14.

The boxer delicately rolled a gentleman-sized joint and retired to his backyard. He splayed his always aching legs across the tile and looked up at the swirling pinkish curls in the light pollution where stars that used to be dying millions of years ago used to be visible. He puffed his cheeks in and out, sending out tiny perfect smoke rings. The boxer shifted his gaze down and started, his head jumping as if to stand before settling back into a serious inhale. Breathing out his nose, Pillow killed the joint and walked inside to violate the sacred confidences of roommates by going straight downstairs and into Sherlock's bedroom without knocking.

Sherlock's pyjamas looked like a swimsuit from when swimsuits were just another pair of weirdly elaborate underwear you air-dried.

'May I assist you, Pillow?'

'You didn't happen to investigate the grounds when we got home, did you?'

His legs looked like two unfolded tent poles in weirdly high socks. 'I did not.'

'Okie dokie, so let's just throw on some pants and meet me in the backyard.'

Sherlock pulled his pants back on and flipped the deerstalker onto his head.

Once they were outside, the roommates stood quietly looking for a while. At a certain point, Pillow reached down and pressed on the bone of his wrist, sending a thick pop through the silence of the night. The giraffe kept her feet perfectly still as her face moved its flesh and teeth purposefully across branch after branch of the crabapple tree, decimating fruit.

Sherlock had been stroking his chin for a long time. 'And you are absolutely confident you did not … '

'I didn't forget buying a giraffe.'

'Mmmmm. But you are acquainted with this giraffe, correct?'

Pillow giggled and punched his roommate kindly under the ribs. 'You are a good fucking detective. Not even just with logic and shit, you're just out here making reads. Yeah, this is Gentleman Jim.'

'I believe this to be a female giraffe.'

'Doesn't mean she's not a gentleman.'

'An unassailable point.'

'She's my girl at the zoo. Every time I go, I pop in and say hi.'

Gentleman Jim had eaten every crabapple on the tree. She looked at the two men drowsily, licked her entire face, and then wandered into the dark.

'It would appear your efforts to divest yourself of your menagerie are not going well.'

Pillow shrugged. 'I got rid of the shark at least.'

Sherlock shivered, and Pillow followed him wordlessly into the house. The detective got his pipe going, and the boxer gamely chugged on a gallon of water.

'So, you're still hired.'

'Sweet Pillow, in the face of interest I am perpetually engaged. It would appear our adventure has taken the turn to mystery. The rules and logics of Lupin's game come more readily into view.'

Pillow fingered around the puffy edges of the hole in his face. 'Mystery or not, I've got some serious business shit to do tomorrow. No games for me. What do giraffes need?'

Sherlock killed his pipe in the sink, then dryly patted Pillow's hand. 'Monsieur Painlevé and I left on exceptionally good terms. The man is a sweet and trustworthy dupe, with some admirable skills as a cutman and animal custodian. I will call him tomorrow to make arrangements.'

Pillow nodded and was thinking about talking about cops and when zoos might call them and how hard it is to hide anything that weighs 1,700 pounds when there was a dopey, hollow thunk on the window. The two roommates turned, arm in arm now, to look at the giraffe's face and the huge streak her wet face and nose were leaving across the glass of Pillow's door, because that's the kind of thing you do when you now live without a shark and with a giraffe.

15.

Kim lifted Pillow's Winnie the Pooh hat off by the little bear ear and made a show of inspecting the back of his head.

'Cut's on the front. What are you looking for?'

She tapped his skull and moved to sit across from him, dropping the hat in his lap. 'I was wondering maybe you wore the hat to cover the hole in your head. Because no motherfucker with even half of a half of a cortex left in his skull is going to slice himself, blow his insurance, when he could have had me step on his ankle, get the fight pushed easy.'

'It was an accident.'

Kim had a picture of herself with the Shah of Iran on her desk that she for some reason treasured. She picked it up and ran her fingers over their faces, took a deep breath, and replaced it. 'What kind of accident leaves a cut like that?'

'I was snuggling a dog. A mastiff.'

She grabbed one of her braids and twisted hard enough to make Pillow wince from watching. Her voice came out as if squeezed from a stiff plastic bottle. 'Go on.'

'I was thinking over what you said. I start feeling in my body like I need to snug a dangerous dog. No Shih Tzu, no Havanese, I've got to wrap up a man-sized dog and feel her heartbeat, feel those dog ribs against me. Right? And this mastiff I was … she just scratched me, caught a patch of scar tissue to get it started, went right through.'

'Fuck. That is kind of what it looks like. This … this is a new one, Pillow. They're gonna love this one.'

'I know.'

'And I know you've got some shady shit going down with that fuckin' roommate of yours. But I'm done asking. You're telling me a story I believe the important part of, I know your sketchy ass well enough to stop asking.'

Pillow poked around the far edge of the cut. 'I've got a plan.'

'This'll be good.'

'I'll tell them the whole thing and convince them. And they'll push the fight.'

'Oh, now he's sure they'll push it.'

Pillow flashed a grin and kept talking. 'They'll push it. And I put 900 pounds of cocoa butter on my face every fuckin' day to be back at the gym, every day. I sleep and dream and maybe even melt and become one with a fuckin' sea of cocoa butter each night. I'm feeling it again. I feel it. If we fight in six weeks, my weight'll be perfect. My legs are already there. No getting in shape, I start in shape and build. I come into this fight with my heart wide open.'

'Heart wide open.' She snorted as effectively as however much of her septum was still in the approximate right place allowed. 'It's your face looks wide open to me.'

Pillow dropped to his hands and knees, crawled behind the desk, and kissed the top of both Kim's army boots. 'I know. I know what it's been. I'm going to pay off, all the shit I put you through. You get the real one this time.'

Pillow sat up to his knees. A smile as reluctant as a wolf at a salad bar moved slowly across her face, finally finding the bacon bits and ham right at the very end. She kicked him in the abdomen, and Pillow didn't flinch.

'All right. I get the real one this time. The real one does what I say? Trains how I tell him to? The real one doesn't blast a line in the parking lot, come in and beat up my amateurs, pretend he's getting ready for a fight?'

'I do whatever you tell me to do, whenever you tell me to do it. Promise.

'Sure. You clear it with Cravan, I'll ride with you.'

Pillow stood and bowed. 'Now let's go train.'

'Are you stupid? Look at your face.'

'Why would you look at my face … ' Pillow ripped his T-shirt clean across the chest with one pull and flexed. 'When these ab insertions are just a layer of cloth away?'

She laughed. 'If you're going to be crazy, may as well be crazy about training.'

'Exactly.'

'Put those cum gutters away, man. Ab insertions are genetic anyhow.'

Pillow did some clapping push-ups, hopped up, and entered Winnie the Pooh from the bottom.

'So's all this talent.'

16.

Pillow had been sitting in a chair as expensive as a liver transplant for what felt like the length of a liver transplant looking at Arthur Cravan look at the cut and hoping that neither of them was seeing the end of his career.

Pillow's promoter, Arthur Cravan, was wearing an entire polar bear's skin over a suit too expensive to remember what seams look like. It didn't really matter what month it was, or that it happened to be a very hot one, because Arthur Cravan was wearing the entire polar bear in an office a decent way up in the sky in a building where every room had its own weather, and, thanks to a thousand invisible vents, the weather in Arthur Cravan's office was cold enough to justify wearing an endangered species as a coat.

Cravan did all the things with his face that a world-renowned doctor who knows only and exactly about cuts would do as he thought about Pillow's cut. The fight promoter raised the bear's arm, opened and closed his delicate human fist. 'So, you're saying you were attacked by a mastiff?'

'No, I told you I was snuggling her. It was an accident. A loving accident between new friends.'

Arthur Cravan's father was a self-made millionaire who'd handed the boxing business off to his son, and Arthur had not yet totally bankrupted that business, so he was a self-made millionaire now too. 'You're telling me I'm going to forfeit my site fees because you hug dogs. Not because all camp all anyone's been talking about is how bad you're looking, how you're not training, looking strung out. It's not because of any of that? It's the dog thing.' Arthur Cravan laughed so hard he coughed into the bear's neck, then used the bear's wrist to wipe the corner of his mouth.

'I know it looks bad.'

'You tell me something looks bad, you're telling me that's not what it actually is. I picked you up off the scrap heap, and you do this to me.'

Pillow looked out a window so big it circled all the way back around to looking like the empty sky. 'My man, you own the scrapyard. You took me in off the street and turned me right back out, made all your money back, don't act like you didn't. I had an accident snuggling with a dog. You push the date a few weeks. You still get your fight, and your golden boy still gets his step-up without getting that sweet little chin tested.'

Cravan let a small grin play at the edge of his mouth. 'I knew it was stupid to let you talk to me without lawyers around. As much as I like you, Pillow, I can get a short-notice replacement for sixty cents on the dollar.'

After he left Boots Frutch, Pillow had worked with a trainer who used to always call things Catch-22s. If you're stuck in the corner, you duck low and you're vulnerable to the uppercut; you pull back straight, you can get caught with the right hand. Put yourself in the corner, you've put yourself in the Catch-22, the trainer said. And, after hearing it a few dozen times, Pillow had looked it up. And it turned out a Catch-22 means that by being fucked one way you are contractually obligated to be fucked some other way. Being in the corner is not a Catch-22, it's a rough spot where every choice has a drawback. There's always something bad about the thing you do, even and especially when you're doing the right thing.

Pillow knew that only a Catch-22 is really a Catch-22. Everything else is just a chance to be slick and look slick doing it. Pillow was an old, barely legitimate challenger for a world title belt that barely meant anything. Although there was no good reason, on paper, to keep him, Pillow knew Cravan was going to do it. Because most of the reasons that matter aren't the good ones.

They're the ones in the room with you. Cravan was looking at Pillow's cut face, hearing the short timeline, and imagining his golden boy's highlight-reel KO.

'Arthur, we're spending all these words, and the whole time we're both sitting here knowing it ends with you saying some numbers and me saying yes.'

Arthur Cravan slid out of the bear as he stood. He said, 'Warm,' and then the room was the temperature of a bath that had been scalding half an hour ago. Cravan circumnavigated his desk, pulled up a chair, and showed Pillow an itemized list of all the money he was taking from him. Pillow read it over.

'You've got me fighting for free.'

'I'd prefer you think of it as fighting for equity. You win this fight, you'll more than make it back on the next one. This is the offer. You blow your insurance, it comes out of your purse. I can't lose money on this one.'

Pillow looked over Cravan's shoulder and saw a picture of a yacht and its pet helicopter an inch away from kissing. 'Book it.'

Cravan clapped and hopped up, patting Pillow on the shoulder. 'Sign beside every sticky note and you've kept your fight.'

Pillow signed beside every sticky note and slumped back in his chair. 'You got it all, hey? The small ring, the judges, the ref, the money. You got everything you wanted.'

'You wanted it too. That's what an agreement is.'

'If you say so. You're the agreement guy. Me, I'm the disagreement guy, so all I've got to say is wait till you get a load of me.'

Cravan picked up the papers and leaned against the desk. 'I do like you, Pillow. You're a sentimental favourite, for what that's worth. But Julio Solis, the Golden Boy, is golden because he dreams his life with great care, instead of living it merely as an amusement. And that's where I'm going to put my money until further notice.'

Pillow flashed his golden tooth. 'See you at further notice.'

17.

Having just signed away more money than he had to keep a fight he was supposed to lose, Pillow weightlessly dropped five hundred feet and exited a building that weighed more than every snowy owl in the world combined. Drifting to the curb, Pillow got hailed by Jean Painlevé before he had a chance to hail a cab.

'Pillow. We have some small intercourse pending.'

The boxer silently dropped his weight and came up under Painlevé's hip, hoisting him over his shoulder. 'The best I can promise is chill, intercourse-wise.'

Painlevé shrugged his shoulders down toward his dangling arms. 'And so chill will do.'

Pillow adjusted his grip to a better spot on the quad. He'd been fooled by how weirdly high Painlevé wore his pants. The little Frenchman's hips could have been just about anywhere. 'Did you bring a car?'

'Of course.'

'Did you bring a race car?'

Painlevé gently tapped the backs of Pillow's knees and hopped back to standing. He tugged the sections of his baggy suit back over the approximate shapes of his body they were supposed to associate with. 'Pillow. Don't we know one another? Would I come for a man like you unprepared to commit a road felony?' A small, fossilized sea horse fell out of his sleeve, and Painlevé kicked it out into the street. 'Forgive my toothpick. Let's hit the road. The wonders of the sea await!'

Painlevé's race car wasn't so much a convertible as a metal tube with four wheels and two side-by-side cockpits. Pillow had asked where he bought it, and Painlevé had wiggled his driving goggles and floored it. They didn't get much talking done as Painlevé weaved erratically between lanes until they reached the countryside, and then weaved as erratically as the bends of the gravel roads allowed. Pillow sat in his cockpit quietly, shielding his gaping cheek against the wind and thinking vaguely about insurance and some other things that can or cannot be re-violated.

Painlevé screeched the car to a stop at a seemingly random spot a seemingly random distance from the sea. He stood up in his seat and waved his entire arm at a wet stick figure. Painlevé tipped back and sat on the rear edge of his cockpit, lazily moving his hand to settle on the crown of Pillow's head.

'I really am sorry, Pillow. It seems I was duped. But being duped is the tax we pay on the ample, eternal salary of our wide open hearts.'

Pillow peeled the hand off his head index finger first. 'Wide open hearts, hey? I was just talking about one of those. Sherlock's been cooking up some Soviet angina drugs for you too.'

Painlevé took off his driving goggles and turned them around, looking up the winding road. 'I wasn't talking about the meldonium. But as an aside he has. No, I mean this Arsène Lupin character. I've steered you wrong. I was tricked in whole cloth. I've never promised skepticism or discernment, or even really good judgment. But I was insufficiently cautious even by my own standards.'

Pillow hoisted himself up, and the two men sat silently for a while, listening to the sea move and watching the road sit still. 'No worries. That's Sherlock's gig now. I'm a fighter. Next few weeks it's head down, eyes clear, heart wide open for me.'

'A mindset I can certainly appreciate.' He flipped his driving goggles onto his seat, pressed down on a metal panel, and grabbed the diving goggles that popped out. 'Let's forget all about how gullible we are and hit the beach. The place where gullibility is rewarded above all other human qualities.'

They walked over to Genevieve. The sky was a luminescent sheet of clouds, so overcast it was completely uniform. It had rained a little bit a long time ago, enough to wet the top of the ground and make the greys of the cold beach rocks pop against the blue of the water. Genevieve was crouching beside a seven-foot-long line of individually laid out scuba and film gear. Painlevé pulled his diving goggles over his eyes and nose and unbuttoned his shirt to reveal a wetsuit that looked like a wrestling singlet.

Genevieve was busy tinkering with some sort of knob attached to some sort of tank. 'I wish you'd called ahead. There's only one suit.'

Pillow reached down and guided one hanging lock of her hair out straight, dropping it across her face. 'Might try looking up.'

'Jesus.' She stood and fingered the edge of his gash. 'What dog scratched you?'

'How'd you know it was a dog?'

She knocked on his collarbone. 'I'm a scientist, dumb-dumb. Wait a tick, I've got something for that.'

Genevieve disappeared over the side of the rock. Pillow turned to see Painlevé holding a giant boxed camera with a plate-glass front out from where his uterus would be if he'd been a person with a uterus. 'Shame you can't come into the depths with me, Pillow, but to wade is almost better. To stand, feet in the water, gazing into this sinister pond to which we all owe everything. It's sublime. Knee-deep, ankle-deep, toes kissing the edge or head stuck in a sea trench. The last thing that matters is depth.' And with that, he took a header off the rock.

Genevieve was back, having created a tide pool in her hands. Pillow saw that she was holding a sea anemone, its green exterior peeled back to show a thousand dangling pink tubes. 'Bring your cheek over here.'

'You're going to put that on my face?'

'I'm here with a creature of the sea forest that will nestle itself lovingly onto you. You trust a dry thread tied around a dry needle held between two latex fingers to go through your face, but you don't trust this little cutie to suck you?'

Pillow crossed his arms and closed one eye. 'You put it like that.' He dipped his head and exposed the cut, and Genevieve nestled the anemone on, letting go as Pillow felt the odd, dry grip of the wet little tubes. Pulling back, Genevieve grinned, held up a finger. The camera was wider than her head and longer than her neck. She clicked away for a while, then nodded to the water.

'Let's show you off to your new lover's extended family.'

Pillow stripped off his shoes and socks. He briefly considered the legs of his pants, and then he took the pants off. They waded into the water and silently walked around for a while, Genevieve pointing out little fish and huge anemones, sometimes kneeling down to stick her finger in one. After a while, they sat down on a wet rock, and Genevieve firmly shoved his face into the water. After a couple seconds the little pink tubes gently released his face, and the anemone sank gratefully onto a rock, jostling in time with the tide. Pillow touched the edges of his cut, which felt healthily moist, hydrated from the inside but dry to the touch, the jagged edges of the gash smooth and linear now. Pillow didn't thank people who didn't want to be thanked, so he just tapped her on the wrist. A hundred feet away, Painlevé's head emerged from the water as if his head were air and the sea were a pump. He leapt up to wave and fell right back down, pulled by the weight of the box of his camera.

18.

Somewhere between a meeting in which he'd given away enough money to fund a small regional public library system for a year and kept a commitment to fist fight a man eight years younger and at least five pounds per weight per rep regardless of the lift stronger than him and getting his cut sucked on by a creature of the sea forest, Pillow had forgotten how he left his house in the first place. Rather than wonder about where things stayed or didn't in his brain, Pillow made Painlevé drive him home. It had been a big day, so Pillow just slumped against the edge of the passenger cockpit, keeping his eyes closed against the brushing kiss of the wind.

Painlevé screeched the car up to the house, and the two men wordlessly went to see the giraffe. Gentleman Jim was roaming as far as the yard allowed. Gangling her legs over in sections, aimlessly poking her head over the side of the security fence, then pulling it back and repeating the gesture at the other side. For once, Pillow was glad his neighbours on either side were shitty enough people to own mansions they didn't live in.

Remembering his driving goggles, Painlevé wiggled them before pushing them back over his pushed-back hair. 'A majestic creature.'

Gentleman Jim began peeing, the liquid falling to the ground as if through a trap door slammed open.

'Are you sure I can't keep her? I mean, she's at a zoo normally, how much worse could it be to … '

Painlevé reached over and held Pillow's wrist with two hands. 'Much, much, much worse.'

'That was a lot of much.'

'I can assure you the volume of much was, if anything, understated, my dear Pillow.' Sherlock had apparently been waiting in the shadows, thin and still enough to seem like another folded-up sun umbrella.

'Tough day?'

Sherlock tapped the ground with his walking stick in perfect time with his finger tapping the tip of his chin. 'It was a full day and an engaging one, in its fashion. I was occupied primarily in solving our case, the specifics of which I will not allow to burden the limited store of that priceless commodity, your attention.'

'Appreciated.'

'The rest of the day, however, was occupied by the sorts of chores that with time and habit become menial but when illuminated by novelty are educational. This giraffe requires approximately seventy-eight pounds of light roughage and fruits each day. We would also be well-advised to acquire new play items to keep the giraffe stimulated in absence of intraspecies social contact.'

Gentleman Jim nosed up to the stripped branch of Pillow's favourite cherry tree, tapping it twice and yearningly pressing the tip of her massive purple tongue to the absence of fruit.

Painlevé was nodding away like a desk toy whose only purpose is to touch but not drink water. 'Sherlock has the thrust of it here, Pillow. To be whatever it takes to be a giraffe humans call sane the animal needs either social contact from a close group of females and a dominant male or an infinite arboretum on which to graze mindlessly until death.'

Pillow rubbed the eye that hadn't been almost clawed out by a mastiff. 'Those are seriously the only options?'

Sherlock and Painlevé exchanged shrugs at each other and then Pillow. 'The only ones worth considering.'

Gentleman Jim slowly coiled down, twisting her head to rest on her rump. The boxer moved toward her, stopping a respectful distance away to look at what her eyes looked like closed. 'Sherlock, you stay on the case. Jean, think you can manage to get more exotic pets out of my house?'

'I'll do my best.'

Pillow nodded and moved to stand over the giraffe. He considered petting her, and then he remembered that reiki is actually kind of real. The boxer ran his hands through the air along the giraffe's ropey, knotted neck, trying to give her the kind of massage that works because sometimes it's better to be nearby thinking about healing than knuckled in deep, beating some muscles that just wanted to be hard together until they're soft and lonely.

19.

Pillow woke up to run, and where he always saw a square, dark window he now saw a square window filled with a giraffe's face. The boxer waved and the giraffe blinked twice and disappeared. He threw on some tights and ran sprints in his driveway; he panted his way inside, had a meldonium and an americano, and then looked at the fractured, ghosty combination of Gentleman Jim eating a bowl of iceberg lettuce tied to the top of the crabapple tree and his own body reflected in the glass as he consumed four consecutive boiled eggs.

Pillow felt it was legitimate to still call himself a vegan with the eggs because chickens need to drop eggs and if you're 100 percent sure that your eggs come from a chicken whose whole life is just walking around in a field and then sleeping with enough space to flap her wings once in a while when she has a nightmare about foxes then all you've really done is enjoy an object someone felt better after ejecting from her body. Milk and cheese weren't at issue because Pillow had always been disgusted by both substances. It was not that Pillow thought that any grown man who drank a full glass of milk should be jailed; it was that we should keep an eye on him.

The boxer weighed himself, shaved, and brushed his teeth, periodically flexing into the wall that was also his bathroom mirror. He listened to music as he stretched and did his ab routine and allowed a muted boxing match to ambiently enter his brain through his eyes. Pillow went downstairs and counted out seven salted almonds and ate them before he drank a smoothie with twenty-eight different objects that used to be parts of living plants and a huge scoop of protein powder that had never been anything but exactly what it was.

He went to the yard and looked up at the empty sky and the sadness of the giraffe's eyes. Painlevé had left a list of stimuli for when the giraffe looked sad, and Pillow looked at it, shrugged, and then turned on some Cuban jazz. Gentleman Jim's sadness seemed to whisk away completely, like a tablecloth pulled by someone who's very confident they won't break everything on the table. The giraffe galloped the few steps the yard allowed, then she did an adorable hop-skip type of thing and wiggled her neck a bit. They played a kind of fetch where Pillow threw a ball and instead of fetching Gentleman Jim would chase the ball and punt it into a fence. Often, the giraffe would step on and obliterate the ball, so Pillow would throw another one.

The only things Pillow really knew about Cuban jazz were that he didn't like jazz all that much and he was ambivalent on Cuban boxers. Cubans had the best amateur boxing program in the world. They had no money, no nothing, but they won just about everything on the amateur circuit.

On the pro side, Cuban boxers tended to disappoint. They came over when they were already old (and probably older than they said) and so confident in their style they wouldn't change it for professional boxing. Cubans were happy to calmly pick and poke and move around the ring, spiking their opponent with straight lefts and thinking they were winning just by looking cool. Cubans would get in there with you and win the first couple rounds, snap your head back a few times, then just stink it out. Pillow had always thought they lacked heart.

But, seeing them through Gentleman Jim's sad giant eyes, Pillow was starting to feel it. He did something between remembering and imagining a room full of Cuban kids training. He saw their slick, slippery footwork, the bouncy arrogant rhythm of the whole thing. He saw that they had something more beautiful than fighters' hearts; they had artists' eyes. The rhythm, the bounce, the dance of it all. And wasn't that a better thing to do than fight?

So that's what he did. An hour straight of casual, low-key bouncing around, slipping and ducking imaginary punches and pivoting around imaginary big toes, and seeing the imaginary counterpunch openings and being too classy to even throw the counter. Gentleman Jim didn't bob her head to the music as she watched, it was more that she let it relax into a gentle sway that you could paint over with rhythm if you wanted.

As he was drinking enough water to drown a kitten, the boxer caught sight of the tails of Sherlock's hunting coat just barely escape the closing door. His man was on the case. Pillow mixed an extremely aggressive preworkout powder into the rest of his water and drank it. He waited on the couch for a while staring into the empty water of his full shark tank, shit explosively, hit the double-end bag for a few rounds, slapped himself until his eyes watered, did 120 push-ups, and then went to the room of his house that was just pictures of himself shirtless and trophies and belts that he'd won shirtless in display cases and stood in there awhile, looking at himself and thinking about himself and drinking enough liquid to waterboard a full-grown man. Pillow's chest felt full, and his head felt light, and he had only as many thoughts in his head as he needed. If he did this exact thing forty-five more days in a row, he would be ready and he would win his fight and he would be back. And the little room in his house that was just pictures of him shirtless and trophies and belts he'd won shirtless in display cases wouldn't be a little room in his house anymore, it would be the whole world.

Pillow went to work, and the person he trusted most in the world hit him in the stomach with a medicine ball two hundred times.

20.

The parking lot Pillow found himself in wasn't anywhere in particular. The baby, on the other hand, was very particularly sitting with diagram-perfect posture on the hood of Gwynn Apollinaire's car.

Apollinaire was reclining over the hood and, as if pulled by a loose silk string, she gradually rose to face Pillow. 'Ah, it's my man. My man with the face. Or what's left of it.'

The baby squawked and smacked the hood with an open palm.

'Listen, Gwynn, I was going to call you. Fight's still on, we're still good.'

Her old flintlock pistol had appeared from somewhere, and Gwynn pointed it straight out at Pillow, then spun it around to rest abruptly against her own forehead. 'Still good. The condition of us being good is still happening, I suppose.' She pulled her forehead tight, jogging the gun barrel before disappearing it again down her confusingly ruffled shirt. 'All that's good in this world, Pillow, is love. And love, like life, is slow. And love, like hope, is violent.'

The baby had been staring Pillow in the eyes the whole time. He briefly met the baby's dogged glance and the baby immediately burst into tears.

Pillow paused to gather his thoughts. Then he pointed at the screaming child. 'Okay, I get that you're a vibe-setter, with the props and the pistols, and style is cool. Style is cool, I … but a baby?'

'You're raising an ethical objection?'

'It's a human baby. I mean, at some point … '

Gwynn reached all the bones of her hand to rest on the child's stomach and it immediately stopped crying and started sucking its middle two fingers. 'How do you know I'm not babysitting my niece? How do you know I wasn't interrupted in my family duties?'

Pillow let out a breath that you might call a laugh. He tilted his head back and looked at a few dozen stars that had been dead for a few million years. 'We both know you've got to roll. Odds are way up now. Nothing changed but the odds, which is good.'

'And how much have you left to wager? To make me feel good.'

Pillow looked back and gestured vaguely at pockets he didn't even have to turn out. 'I'm tapped.'

The baby was still staring at him, concertedly sucking her middle two fingers. Apollinaire scooped up the baby and kissed her behind the ear. The baby didn't react, except to reposition her non-sucking hand on Apollinaire's bony shoulder. The gangster spoke without looking. 'And what, really, Pillow is the difference between zero and infinity?'

'I guess I'll be finding out.'

Apollinaire kissed the baby's head. 'No, no, no. No more fucking around, my friend. You don't guess anything. You know what you've been knowing for some time now.'

21.

Sometimes, for reasons he'd never fully understood, Pillow was supposed to encase his hands in paraffin wax. The whole process took an hour, between heating the wax, dipping, and then sitting still with his hands suspended in the air waiting until he was allowed to peel his new skin away. He'd had another good day at the gym, another day with his body bumping successfully into other bodies and bags of sand he was pretending were bodies. So, he was getting updated on his business affairs. Being informed.

Painlevé was talking about how hard it is to find an ethical giraffe sanctuary. Sherlock was lying flat on the marble floor tracing the bloodless tips of his fingers over the veinless track marks of his arms. There were a few fresh ones on there, so Pillow knew there wouldn't be any great updates on that end.

'Just to clear the air, why the fuck am I not already arrested for having this stolen giraffe?'

Painlevé was calibrating a monocular telescope by pointing it directly into the light. He pulled the device away from his eye, blinked a few times, wiggled a dial, and put the thing down at the marble lion's paws. 'It would appear that you have an eye for giraffes, Pillow. Our friend Jim happens to be a giraffe acquired under nebulous circumstances by the zoo and was consequently something less than logged in their system. You have a stolen giraffe, but the zoo will insist it was not stolen from them.'

'Right, right. Don't I need a permit to own a giraffe?'

'I think it has been assumed that anyone rich enough to own a giraffe is also the proud owner of a permit to do whatever the fuck they want forever and ever.'

'Right, right. Okay, so how about moving her?'

'That's trickier. As you know, I've been recently duped by a buyer so I'm trying new methods. Results pending.' He winked.

'Why are you winking at me?'

'Oh sorry.'

Pillow brought his wax fingertips together, turned to face Sherlock. 'What about you, mystery man? You're out there making money moves?'

Sherlock rolled languidly onto his elbow. 'I am neither being paid for my labour nor spending money to accomplish it. My work at present is mental, and as such I am not moving terribly much.'

'So, you're sitting still in your room thinking.'

'That is correct. I am almost ready to reveal to you the solution to this problem. There is one missing element for which I must account, and it is vexing me to the point of torture.'

Pillow had been back training hard for the past week. And, for most of that time he had felt the way an eagle looks with 5,000 feet of air under its wings, and for the small rest of the time he'd felt the way a salmon feels with any distance of air under its gills.

The soundest lesson boxing teaches is that there are no free rides. It's not that everything balances out, it's just that highs are always punished. Training this way gave Pillow access to the perfect exact feeling: when you train hard on just enough food, take a cold shower, and put on a crisp, clean shirt. Empty, cleaned out, glowing. Like life is a giant newspaper spreading out in front of you. And, to Pillow, that feeling was worth it, a feeling too perfect to be deserved. So, you also had times like this. Times where the strength of your body turns suddenly into weight. Where the beautiful tight corners of your muscle turn into ropes of pain and exhaustion tying your body to whatever happens to be around.

Pillow happened to be on a couch he'd bought knowing how very often he'd have to make himself feel this bad to keep paying for couches this nice. He folded himself slowly onto his back, his wax hands extended straight above him, looking like a pen drawing of Frankenstein's monster turned on the narrow edge. 'What have you found out?'

Sherlock sat up, his legs shooting out in front of him like an easel collapsing unexpectedly. 'A thief as seemingly spontaneous as our dear Arsène Lupin is always in the act of planning. He is a seeker of public attention, as are we all in the folly of our youth. After his arrest, Lupin made some noise about his retirement from thievery due to its decreasing difficulty and intellectual interest. A retirement I believe entirely sincere.'

'If he's so sincere about it, where's my fucking car?'

Sherlock sighed. 'You have hit precisely on the only sore point available. I do not know. The car does not fit with my theory. On all the other spots, I can explain to a deductive certainty. Absent the car there is a clear, if unconventional, logical thread. True thievery involves not just stealing but keeping. And it is this act that has lost its appeal to Lupin. It is too easy to take a cherished object, so he's found the best way to complicate the exercise.'

'Putting something back.'

'Precisely, sweet Pillow. Precisely. Taking, putting back, and adding. You have now a pet you'd only coveted. A pet he stole that was already stolen, a pet he returned to the owner she'd never had but always deserved.' Holmes rose to his feet, puffed his chest out and set to pacing. 'In other words, we are not chasing a thief, we are chasing the purveyor of far deeper crimes against society's fellowship.'

'Which is?'

'A philanthropist.'

22.

Kim was hosting a smoker at the gym, so Pillow's schedule had been flipped, and he'd gotten in his gym work early in the morning and headed home for his conditioning. Sherlock was out and about, so Pillow had taken his lunch in the yard, watching Gentleman Jim graze over a series of apples tied to a branch as the boxer drank enough water to boil a human torso in. Then he held two full droppers of THC tincture Sherlock had prepared for him under his tongue until they were spit.

Pillow did two hundred crunches and pulled a rusty iron sled back and forth across his lawn twenty times, took his pulse, did fifty burpees and ten plyo push-ups, then curled into a small ball on the ground and fantasized about being a tiny pebble at the beginning of a stream whose water would end up storming over Niagara Falls.

He returned to the backyard to stretch, Cuban jazz tinkling through the air as he watched Gentleman Jim glumly poke her nose into the dry sticks where there had used to be apple blossoms. Pillow loved giraffes, but if pressed he would have to admit that having one as a pet was a letdown. Practically, it was a huge hassle. She cost an amount of money to care for that was, even to Pillow's eye, an issue. She smelled really, really bad. And, most importantly, Gentleman Jim had a problem with sadness. After initially seeming content with the trees and everything, playing with the beach balls, running her little laps, Gentleman Jim had gotten down in the dumps. She spent most of the day lying down, all coiled up on herself, head rested sadly on rump. She moved slowly, and the very top of her neck drooped down a little. She spent the afternoons standing in front of the side wall, tapping the tip of her nose against the concrete in the same, dull metronomic pattern, like a woodpecker with a mitten tied over its beak. Pillow picked up a bright red bouncy ball, turned his back, and threw it as far as he could over his shoulder.

The boxer went inside and tamped down a physical hunger that gnawed to the core of his being by drinking enough water for a dolphin to give birth in and chewing a large stick of gum to dust. He went to his bedroom and watched his entire career from start to finish. Pillow had most of his fights on video, whether they were television broadcasts or grainy footage of club fights. He sat still and watched himself box for four and a half hours straight. He decided to start at the end.

By the end, which was the beginning, he liked what he saw. And he knew, now, what he needed to do. It's great to be slick, to have the full bag of tricks. But the point of a bag of tricks is to pull one out when you need it, not to just dump the whole thing out on the table every time. While he'd been getting smarter and craftier, Pillow had been losing something. As he watched his twenty-year-old self dip and shuck and bounce and clown around the ring, keeping the distance and closing to fire off flashy strings of pitty-pat punches, he knew that he needed the volume back, the activity. This fight wasn't about laying traps. It was about initiative. Setting the tone, making the kid fight off the back foot, feinting and throwing. Energetic, engaged, and doing his thing. Not watching and waiting and picking and poking but taking centre once in a while, making it happen for himself.

He flexed his right hand, which had the empty buzzing quality a hand that always hurts has when it is right that second not hurting because of how much THC tincture you had under your tongue a few hours ago. Pillow knew that this time he'd have to really throw it. He'd have to let the right hand go. Because there was no other fight to save it for. It might hurt, and he'd probably break the hand again, but this time he'd keep throwing it after it was broken. This was a promise Pillow had made to himself three times before. The first time his hand had held up and he'd won his first title. The next time the hand had shattered as cleanly and enthusiastically as a thin sheet of ice at the bottom of a freezer, and the time after that it had crumpled like a car fender whose whole purpose on this earth is to fold in on itself when the time came.

Onscreen, his first fight finally ended, and Pillow watched his tiny-shouldered, barely-not-a-child self peer up at the guy filming him and wink a bloodshot eye. Pillow smiled back at a kid who knew exactly what was coming next, whose hands felt like weapons and whose body felt like a fully charged car battery about to get a jump. He used that kid's right hand, which now felt less like a weapon and more like the serial number filed off a weapon he'd bought in a Wendy's parking lot, to punch himself a few times in the head. He did a backwards roll, hopped up, threw a thirty-punch flurry, and then screamed at the top of his lungs and listened to the sound a mansion makes after someone has screamed and nobody but the giraffe in the yard was home to hear it.

Pillow's biggest worry wasn't that they wouldn't find a good home for Gentleman Jim. Enough money, he could find a place. Pillow was worried that Gentleman Jim didn't want a good home, a nice place with other giraffes to love. He was worried that all Gentleman Jim wanted was a place to lie down. A sad place it was easy to be sad in. The drum and guitar started back up, and Pillow decided to dance, and it went the way it always did. He had about three minutes of dancing in him before he started shadowboxing. Firing soft, pillowy punches into the air, and slipping all the imaginary haymakers headed back at him. His eyes closed, his shadow somewhere way off to the side, stretching toward the dark.

23.

As his training intensified, Pillow's grip on the precise schedule and events of his life loosened comfortably, the way your hand does a few minutes into a close walk with someone you love. He finished his conditioning and drank an amount of water that felt, for the first time in a while, reasonably proportioned to his body. The boxer splayed across the floor of his living room, stretching shirtless and admiring his body in the mirror of his rear window as somewhere in the distance Gentleman Jim slumpingly banged her nose against the fence.

He did not immediately notice the shark shimmying hungrily against the glass a foot away from his head for quite some time. It was only after he heard himself passively acknowledge him by name that Pillow remembered Rigoberto was supposed to be missing. With his fight coming up, genuinely motivated now, Pillow was in the business of seeing and reacting. Until he was done fighting Julio Solis stripped to the waist in front of a few thousand people for money, he would not be wasting time thinking smart things. He would spend his time being smart, which is doing smart things immediately without talking about them.

Sharks don't get fat, so Pillow went to the meat freezer and dropped a large portion of a once ethically raised cow that had been processed into a couple dozen paper-wrapped packages. You don't need to bother with defrosting or removing the paper since a shark's teeth are strong enough to eat a licence plate and its stomach is caustic enough to process also a licence plate.

Gentleman Jim had come over to the window and gently nosed up to the glass, leaving another slug's trail of ambient spit streaked across. Pillow grabbed a banana for himself and peeled it and left the peel on the other because animals know what food means better than people do. He slid the back door open and stood with the unpeeled banana above his head, letting some combination of his friend's long disgusting tongue and huge floppy gums settle over his hand. The two rangy omnivores chewed together in silence until there was no more banana meat left, and Pillow reached up to let the floppy gums and weirdly square teeth take his peel. Owning a giraffe was turning out to be small bummer, but Gentleman Jim was the most effective garburator Pillow had ever used. The one in his kitchen was worth eight thousand dollars, and you still needed to call the guy to clear sludge out of it once a year.

The boxer went upstairs, showered, changed, weighed himself, and spent a solid fifteen minutes finding and plucking stray hairs the waxing girl had missed on his shoulders. He moseyed downstairs and found Sherlock, 20,000 bowls of shag tobacco deep, sitting rock still on a chair in an empty room, processing information. The room was somehow hotter than the rest of the house.

'I've got to go. Gentleman Jim will need, shit, like a barrel of apples in a couple hours, and I've fed the shark.' He banged the door jamb with an open hand.

Sherlock exhaled calmly and savagely through his nose. 'The shark?'

'Oh yeah, the shark's back.'

'Interesting.'

Pillow was thinking about the difference between a long body-weight warm-up and banging it out fast with kettlebell activators. 'I suppose it is. Good luck with that.'

'Pillow.'

'Yeah.'

Sherlock stood and came over, grabbing Pillow firmly and gently around the elbow, like a mechanical claw that had gained sentience by downloading twenty-five hundred years of human thinking about kindness. 'That part of me that is most mediocre and true is a hired hand. I appreciate or disdain an indifferent client depending exclusively on the motivation underlying that indifference. One possible driver of apathy is fear and resentment of the skills one needs but must pay to have wielded on one's behalf. And the other is simple trust.' The detective disengaged and extended his bone-dry hand for a warm, limp handshake. 'I trust you as well, my dear friend.'

Pillow had two hours of great training and ten rounds of great sparring. In one of those great rounds Stacks clipped him behind the ear with a hook, and just because it's how brains work some stupid times, Pillow became conscious two hours later, sitting cross-legged on the giant foam pad where Gentleman Jim slept.

In that time, he'd sparred two more rounds, cooled down on the double-end bag, stretched, driven himself home in the rental car, and consumed half a litre of water. And, to everyone who'd seen him, he seemed fine. But it had only been his body talking, driving, and hydrating. In his mind, there was blank space.

These are things you know will happen when you're a boxer with a brain, when you're still a boxer who still has a brain. So, he knew he should get up and walk around. He knew he should call his doctor and take a whole bunch of Advil and get scheduled for a scan.

Instead, he lay down in the empty space between Gentleman Jim's chest and legs and thought about right hands and time and where all the things you can't touch go when you lose them.

24.

Pillow floated through a few more days that were more like collections of tiny wounds. He'd hit something of a middle ground, past the initial point of re-finding the gift of his talent and body, but far short of the burned-out husk of himself he'd been a few weeks ago. Rather, Pillow was at a point where every minute didn't feel like a gift or a punishment, but more like sitting quietly with a cup of tea. He could decide comfortably and unemotionally that it didn't really matter what he did in the long run. So, he should just do all the things he was supposed to.

Pillow came home not hoping but only knowing he would now do the non-things he was supposed to. He would sit quietly, doing nothing while cocoa butter soaked into the folding skin around his cut. He wouldn't go anywhere and he wouldn't talk to anyone and he wouldn't sleep until the time he was supposed to do. And then he wouldn't dream, because remembering your dreams takes some small amount of energy from somewhere.

Sherlock Holmes, on the other hand, had been Doing Things. The detective was pacing the hallway, in the middle of rehearsing a rousing speech. 'Pillow! Your timing is impeccable as always.'

The boxer dropped his gym bag and kicked it away. Pillow had been given no fewer than eight promotional gym bags and sixty T-shirts a year for the last decade. So, in the dog days of camp, that meant he could create a boneyard of gym bags and pay someone money to face it later. He locked eyes with Sherlock and winced, feeling the tug at the healing edges of his cut, and gestured for Sherlock to follow him into the kitchen as the detective said things.

After talking for a while, the sleuth snatched his hat off the table, flipped it up, and let it land slightly askew along the narrow, curving edge of his head. 'Would you like to come along?'

Pillow grunted through a swig of water that accidentally followed a somehow hard layer of air down his esophagus. 'Come where now?'

'To visit Arsène Lupin in prison.'

'Fuck.' He looked out into his yard, and at his giraffe slumped sadly against the fence, which was not even a tall thing she could have hoped had fruit on it. It was just a thing to take on a little of her weight for a while. 'I would.'

Pillow found himself staring out the window of a train that moved as smoothly as a piece of Styrofoam on the surface of a dying river.

'Do not allow yourself to get too settled, Pillow. Our undivided attention is required.'

Pillow wasn't going to get into it right then, but it's very difficult to give your undivided attention to anything when you're less than two weeks out from a professional fist fight. 'So, is he arrested because of this shit? Like the animals and all. Did we file a police report?'

Sherlock squeezed his dry tear ducts. 'No. As previously mentioned, Lupin was arrested on active warrants dating back several years. He has, in fact, been incarcerated since before Violet Hunter came to us, and before any of your animals or possessions dis- or reappeared. Our attention is required because in all likelihood Lupin allowed himself to be arrested in order to make his escape. And has been escaping and returning to his cell for some time.'

'Right, because he's too cool and fancy for stealing now?'

'Indeed, indeed.' Sherlock stood anxiously, looking toward the door like a dog whose owner grabbed the leash before putting on shoes. 'Our stop approaches.'

Pillow pushed himself gradually to his aching feet. 'We don't have to walk to the prison, do we?'

Sherlock gently pushed Pillow out toward the aisle a couple steps, which prompted the boxer to shove off his friend's arm and give him a hard look. Sherlock backed up and made a surrendering gesture, and Pillow continued toward the door.

'No, arrangements have been made to escort us to and from the facility, and our visit will not be officially recorded, since the authorities are not yet in the business of documenting the undead's role in law enforcement.'

A black car with black windows took them to a white building with barred windows. They passed through some hallways with clear gates stronger than brick walls, and once in a while a loud buzz went off and empty space in front of them opened into more empty space they walked through until they had to wait for another buzz. Finally, they entered a room with a thin, long-haired man lying on a bed. A French-looking and low-key-hot-in-an-aristocrat-sort-of-way guy.

Sherlock nodded at the prison warden whose face was a champagne glass too thin to wash by hand, and the warden nodded at the guard whose face was the best mug produced by an adult intermediate ceramics class, and they left the room, locking the door thickly behind them.

Arsène Lupin looked a lot like an empty whitewater kayak whose emptiness is what keeps it from tipping over. The thief rolled to the side of the bed and planted his feet airily on the ground. The room was completely empty except for Lupin, his bed, and a table in the middle. On the table, a boiled egg, a cigar, and an entire grilled swordfish.

Lupin finally looked up. 'There's a way I imagine a man who's lost his shadow must feel. And I don't feel that way. I feel very much in possession of my shadow.' He moved his hand vaguely in front of his face, as if trying to see through it to the floor. 'It's an honour to meet you again, Mr. Holmes.'

Holmes eyeballed Lupin another second, then moved over to the table. He shook his head slightly, cracked the egg, and rolled it across the table, unpeeling it in one long sheet. He handed the eggshell to Pillow and tossed the egg to Lupin, who caught it in his mouth. The eggshell said: 'Museum of Natural History, 3 a.m, skylight.'

Pillow had seen a really good exhibit at that museum about the woolly mammoth and how hard it is to live through an ice age. He felt for the first real time in this whole Lupin thing legitimately affronted. 'Hey, you can't be stealing fossils. That's fucked up.'

Lupin laughed out a crumb of egg yolk.

Sherlock patted Pillow on the shoulder. 'No, dear Pillow, our friend Lupin has no desire to go anywhere near the Museum of Natural History.'

The kayak bumped into a rock, spun around, and lay down, letting the bow go first. 'I am Arsène Lupin. I am that name. So, the authorities here keep giving me allowances. Like these decadent meals brought from outside. They're hoping to fool me into revealing a plot. In return, I feed them a steady diet of action and trinkets. Which can substitute for meaning if you've got the style for it. If you were determined enough to pull the eyes out of that swordfish, you'd find GPS coordinates to a garbage dump outside of town where every crow for 200 miles congregates every evening for some reason that not even determined scientists who think only about birds know.'

Pillow felt very tired, a little bit because he'd burned 5,000 calories that day and mostly because it's so hard to do anything in this world but fail or show off.

Lupin considered standing and rolled on his back. 'I assume Sherlock here has mapped out my every little move. The smuggling myself out and in, the Violet Hunter ruse. I must say that I did not intend for the dog to attack you. Confined as I was to these spartan quarters, I was unable to assure the safety of the play area and the behaviour of my accomplice, and I apologize deeply.'

Sherlock moved to stand over Lupin. 'A bit clumsy.'

Lupin nodded. 'Time, which is to say everything, flies when you're having fun, and it's no coincidence that birds die much more quickly than everybody else.' He crossed his arms behind his head. 'Why should I retain a definite form and feature? Why not avoid the danger of a personality, and leave some part of it to what will happen?'

Pillow wanted to go home. 'And what will happen could be Violet Hunter getting her face eaten by a fucking mastiff.'

Lupin sniffed. 'A gentleman confronts fate with a smile.'

'I guess gentlemen are real pieces of shit. Where did you take Rigoberto?'

'Was he ever gone?'

'Where's my car?'

'What car would that be, exactly?'

Pillow eyed Lupin posed coyly on the bed, a mirthless aesthetic grin tugging at the corners of his mouth. 'My man, I do not give two shits what you did or how cute it was or what the word *gone* means or what *exactly* does to that sentence or any of this other jerk-offy bullshit. I fist fight for a living. I care about what's in front of me and what I can do about it. Are you going to help us get the shark and the giraffe to good homes?'

'I wouldn't have the faintest clue where to start.'

Sherlock raised his hand to jump in, ready to tuck in for all his follow-up questions. Ready to be a detective. Pillow grabbed the swordfish by the tail and lofted it at Arsène's bed. The thief wiped a gill off his cheek and let the rest of the dead fish slide and settle into the crook between his arm and his waist.

'Aren't all of life's efforts diversions? Isn't what's in front of you just as illusory as the wildest fictions of your mind? Mr. Pillow, I do not know you very well, but Sherlock, I'm sure, is well aware of the fact. Is it really so bad to want to look over a cliff with an old rival, just to make sure you've both still got what it takes to jump?'

'You keep calling me mister I'm going to slap the shit out of you.'

Sherlock nodded at Pillow. Then he thought another second and removed his hat, putting it on the table. He turned his back on Lupin. 'It is said that a chess master thinks fifty moves ahead of a novice. This is a thing we say to help us feel that mastery is both possible and beyond our grasp. The truth, however, is that the chess master does not see fifty moves ahead, he sees a move, two, three ahead, and sees them sketchily. No, what makes the chess master different from the novice is not some intricate woven plan stitched upon the inside of his skull and impressed into the welcoming surface of the world. The chess master simply sees fewer options. He is able, without thought, to dismiss thousands of possibilities that addle the mind of the amateur. He sees how few true choices there are, and it is these few, and these few alone, upon which he is able to focus the whole of his being.' Sherlock slipped his arm around Pillow's waist, and they started leaving the room. 'Neither Lupin nor I bested anyone, we each did what we know. He committed no crime, and he knew that I would eliminate all options in which no crime occurred, returning to them when all relevant theories proved inadequate. No one bested anything. We each played our cards, as the kids say, according to Hoyle.'

'Sherlock, you … you're really out of touch with what kids say.'

They called for the guard, and a few seconds later the best mug an adult intermediate ceramics class could ever hope to make popped into a small glass box in the middle of a big steel door.

25.

'Dearest Pillow, I have been appropriately overengaged inquiring on your behalf and I have neglected the other side of my professional obligations to you.'

Pillow was wearing a frozen metal mask the exact shape of his face, and it was very painful to open his eyes or breath or talk. Something about swelling and shock proteins and the massive, healing gash on his cheek. He held up one finger, removed the mask in three tiny, ginger movements, fell to his knees, screamed, and forearm smashed himself where a lit-up nerve was going from his eyebrow to his brain stem.

'Perhaps I have picked an inopportune moment to raise this with you.'

Pillow very carefully peeled the layer of plastic skin he'd been wearing over his cut off to let the mouth of the cut breathe. 'No, I'm good.'

Sherlock tilted his head to one side, looking at Pillow's face like it was a chalkboard with an incorrect equation on it. 'I shall prepare you a mild sedative and analgesic mixture. We can discuss the issue later.'

Pillow hopped to his feet. 'What do I have to do to prove to you I'm ready to hear whatever probably shitty news you have?' He began a stilted, long-legged approximation of a very difficult tap dancing routine, finishing it off with a balletic leap.

Holmes smiled and laid the bones of his hand out toward the chair facing him. Pillow sat down, feeling the no-warm-up leap in his hip flexors.

'I have no news for you, Pillow, good or bad, merely a question. As I was saying, this troublesome affair with your animals and the extremely distressing loose thread of your still missing car has led me to forget some of my obligations as your doping chemist. And so, I must ask if you have been following the instructions I left for you with regards to your regime to beat drug tests for this upcoming contest.'

'The what now?'

Holmes tented his fingers and spoke to his kissing pinkies. 'Since you do not remember the existence of these written instructions, which I know for a fact to be on your bedside table, I shall assume you have not followed the protocol.'

Pillow felt a bit dumb, but he also knew that if you're feeling dumb you're wise enough to know yourself. 'I got caught up. I'm training real hard, there's been all this shit … I just lost track of it, man, sorry. I do remember now your talking about it.'

Holmes nodded gravely. 'I had anticipated just such an eventuality, and thanks to the surprisingly eclectic nature of our dear friend Jean Painlevé's scientific milieu, we have a solution, albeit a risky one.' Holmes loosely unfolded his arm at Painlevé, who had been sitting silently in the corner of the room making shadow puppets on the wall. Painlevé turned a shadow camel into a friendly wave.

'I don't like the sound of that.'

Painlevé hopped to his feet. 'Come now! You should love the sound of it. *Risk* is a wonderful word. Rolls off the tongue. Such a treat.'

About half of being a boxer is making things happen. Getting out there and acting in the blink of the eye with full confidence. About the other half is staying perfectly still and letting people do awful things to your body. Pillow was already strapped to the table. As always seemed to happen when he had all four limbs restrained, random parts of his body lit up with soul-penetrating itches.

Sherlock was at his workbench, pouring liquids into beakers and then putting some of those beakers on tiny, perfect metal stands over tiny perfect blue flames. Painlevé was standing beside Pillow, turning a hand crank and angling the table slowly backwards until it was flat. He patted Pillow's shoulder. 'Fear is nothing but excitement that wasn't hugged enough as a child. Don't worry.'

'How was worry's childhood?'

'Worry is planning deprived of a humanist education.'

Pillow let out a long, loud breath. 'So, just run it by me one more time.'

Painlevé clapped. 'Due to your noted criminal associations, your opponent has requested more than the standard battery of tests, down to the latest in carbon isotope work. So, we must remove all traces of all the very lovely drugs Sherlock has been providing to boost your mood and fitness. Since blood doping is extremely effective in your field of athletics, all the preferred methods of cleaning your blood are themselves detectable by the very tests for which we would be cleaning your blood in the first place. And so, a more avant-garde approach is required.'

'I'm aware of the context, motherfucker. How does this actually work and how sure are you that I won't die?'

Painlevé did an extremely worrying flex of his neck muscles and tendons. 'Confidence, I'm afraid, is not the provenance of true science. Science is fiction written on the beautifully lined foolscap of nature. The key here twirls in Sherlock's beakers, where he is mixing a revolutionary serum originally concocted by a monstrous figure of earth-raping colonialism, one Major General Dr. Léon Normet. This serum, while not a full substitute for blood, substitutes instead the connective functions blood plays in your body. Using Dr. Normet's serum, we will keep you alive and thriving for the relatively short length of time required to exsanguinate you, whoosh your beautiful blood through a very thoughtfully conceived filtration device of Sherlock's invention, and pump you back full of almost exactly as much blood as you had in the first place.'

'I'm going to have all the blood drained out of my body, and you think I should be excited about it?'

Painlevé raised both hands, showing his palms as if his niece had caught him cheating at Monopoly. 'You're a man of art and craft, and I'm a man of science who did badly enough in school to know that art and craft will always matter just a bit more. If I were you, I would be excited. I've always wanted to be one of science's only true winners: the guinea pigs.' He looked over at Sherlock, who pushed his weird giant goggles up to his forehead and flashed four fingers. Painlevé turned back to Pillow. 'See, if science is beautiful it is so because science is not something we do, it's something that is. It doesn't matter who did the science, because if you did the science you simply watched it and noted it down and bragged about it later. The subject gets to be it and to feel it. And if science can make life mean anything, that's who it means it to.' He clapped and then snapped his fingers. 'If that doesn't do the trick, you can always console yourself with the fact that it's the only remote hope you have of passing these drug tests.'

'And this has worked before?'

'On a dog, yes. I can show you the footage.'

'A dog?'

'But there is no reason it shouldn't work on a human being. It should work better. In theory.'

'And the dog's fine?'

'Better than fine, by all reports his mood and behaviour are vastly improved.'

The boxer rotated his neck and tried to enjoy the sickening crunch it always made at the end. 'Fuck it. Drain me.'

Sherlock wheeled over an IV rig and metal table with a bunch of beakers on it. Pillow would have been more comfortable with bags, but it seemed late to fuss over that kind of detail. So much training changes the way your brain works; Pillow did not feel the inclination to close his eyes and tense up when he was scared for his life. Instead, his eyes locked open and his muscles relaxed, ready as always to take pain professionally. He felt the sting as they swabbed his neck with a numbing agent, and a few seconds later he felt the absent poke of the needle into his carotid. Then gravity stopped working on every liquid on the planet while his body stayed where it was and the world got darker, and right before it went black he felt his arms jolt against the restraints, which is a thing your body does as your brain turns off just in case your brain is being turned off by something that's light enough to push away.

It's called a fencing response, and all the people who ever died in a boxing ring have done it.

26.

Pillow's eyes rocked open with the perfect penetrating confidence that he'd been dreaming he was alive and was waking up dead. He took two deep breaths and realized it was the other way around.

Painlevé had been waiting so long he'd moved a more comfortable chair into the room. It was one of the pink fur dining chairs, which were another set of things that had cost Pillow more money than a fast-food manager makes in a year and that he'd forgotten was in the storage closet.

'I died, didn't I?'

Painlevé put one hand over his heart. 'We made a tiny one of what in the scientific profession is known as a whoopsie-doodle-doo. So, yes, you were technically dead for a few seconds. But we reanimated you, and now you can say that you are something not inconsequentially more than alive.'

Pillow felt a bit dizzy and turned his head to see a beaker of his blood beside him feeding into an IV and realized that he was still probably a quart low. 'Maybe I'm not so much like a dog then.'

'No, no, no. That particular bit of comparative anatomy was sound. It occurs to me now that some of the ingredients for the serum may have been a touch less than fresh, which caused an ever-so-slight delay in the onset of the serum's effects.'

'That's occurring to you now, huh?'

'Not to worry. No lasting damage was done. You'll pass these drug tests with soaring colours. We also oxygenated your blood slightly, so once it's back in you there should be a real positive uptick in your training and mood.'

'What about my behaviour?'

Painlevé laughed formally and slapped his knee. 'Your behaviour is your own. And may be as good or bad as you'd like to call it.'

Pillow felt like he'd been sitting on his foot and was just now moving it except his foot was his whole body. He flexed his hands, which moved and then hurt, and wiggled his toes, which moved and felt grateful. 'I just got fuckin' made undead to beat a drug test for a fight I'm not getting paid for. I'm going to skip thinking about what to call myself for a while.'

Painlevé patted Pillow's tingling knee. 'As you recover, I'll tell you a quick story. Once, I was very desperate to be beneath the sea long enough to film octopi making love. When octopi make love, the male reaches a tentacle into the hole through which the female breathes and he leaves dozens of small packets full of his fuck, and then he takes the tentacle out, wiggles it a little, and puts it right back into the poor girl's lungs and rips the packets open. That's physical lovemaking for octopi. There were no air tanks available for my dive, so I rigged a little something up that pumped air into my helmet with a hand crank and I hired a burly father-son duo to crank for my life. And right as the male octopus, white with terror, reached his tentacle toward his lover's gaping lungs, I realized that both of my eyes were about to explode. I dashed for the surface, never so desperate for anything in my life. And what do you think I saw when I got up there?'

'A broken air hose?'

'A father and a son arguing over the most efficient way to work a crank. There's a lesson there.'

'Which is?'

Painlevé looked off to Sherlock lining up all the vials where all of Pillow's blood had been. Ready to rinse. 'Something about work and friendship and things you only miss when they're missing.'

27.

Since he'd had all the blood drained out of his body the night before, Pillow felt it was reasonable to take a day off from training. He didn't even do his miles; instead, he moved between sitting and lying down in his bed, grazing on fruit and drinking water and electrolytes and cups of green tea as his body slowly built some red blood cells. Eventually he called Violet Hunter.

Sherlock had been so fixated on the loose end of the case, Pillow's still missing car, that he'd forgotten the only loose ends that mattered: the ones from all the beautiful hair that Violet Hunter had been tricked into cutting off.

Violet picked up as if surprised by the fact of a ringtone. 'Hello?'

'Hey! It's Pillow.' She didn't say anything immediately. 'Sherlock's roommate, the boxer.'

Violet Hunter laughed breathily into the phone. 'Ooooh, that Pillow. How's your face, dude?'

Pillow had briefly forgotten about the career-threatening gash, and he patted it absently. 'Oh that? It's totally fine. They pushed the fight back, so it's all good.'

'You know that would be, like, the worst injury they've ever had for a lot of people, right?'

'It's not so bad; I think a broken toe is worse. This is just cosmetic, and I'm a butterface anyhow, so it's all good.'

She angled the phone a bit before laughing this time. 'Haven't heard that one in a while.'

'I've got the day off. You up for a marg?'

'I'd do a walk in the park.'

'Here's the thing about a park … '

'Oh goodie, I love being told the thing about things.'

'If it had any balls, it'd be a zoo.'

Painlevé had been right about the oxygenated blood. Pillow had a pep in his step he hadn't had since Stacks had clipped him in sparring. Everything felt fresh and quick and clear, even the zoo had new light to it, as if he were watching the world as a movie with the green turned up. They hit the outdoor animals in a wide meandering loop as Pillow filled Violet in on the end of the case and his upcoming fight and Violet filled Pillow in on the awkward stages of growing your hair back and how weird it feels to write advertising copy about yourself teaching children and a rhinoceros parted his giant flesh-covered plates to shit and a monkey looked Pillow in the eye and masturbated viciously.

Violet was wearing a loose blue shirt that seemed to be buttoned at random places and otherwise flowed in the wind. Her hair had grown back to just past shaved-head level, the ends flirting with the idea of curling. She needed a break from the sun, and they ducked into the Australasian Pavillion because Pillow misremembered the chimps being in there.

She peeked over both shoulders then ran her finger over the glass, scaring a sea horse into changing colour to match the rock behind it.

'I'm telling teacher.'

'You're telling teacher right now, buddy, and don't you forget it.' She looked back at the sea horses. 'You really can't not like an animal with *pot-bellied* in the name.'

'I almost bought a pot-bellied pig one time.'

'Why didn't you? They're cuter than sharks.'

'They're cute as fuck. I was lined up to get one, but when you're laying out five grand for an animal, they let you try him out for a week. So, I got The Mongoose home … '

'You named your pig The Mongoose?'

'He didn't really answer to it. I got him home for a week, and the thing about pigs is they're cute, but they don't do anything for themselves, for real. Like, they need to walk, and you have to walk them, but they absolutely will not keep up with you. They'll keep a five-foot radius snuffling the ground walking like six inches a minute. They're terminally fucking annoying to take care of. And the shit. The shit is … it's … pigs are super similar to humans with their bodies and what they're made of, if you know what I mean.'

'You're talking to a woman who has cleaned up freshly laid human child feces, my man.'

Pillow turned to the sea horse, which was back to a neutral, stripey green colour, galloping floatily across the tank. 'A sea horse: no teeth, no stomach. You're just roaming the sea, mouth-tube out sucking in everything you need, spitting back what you don't. Pot belly right out there, no fucks given. Once in a while, your girlfriend comes over, gets you pregnant. That's a life right there.'

'The males give birth, right. I forgot about that. You know a lot about sea horses.'

Pillow winked into his reflection. 'Oh yeah, I'm learned as shit. I like to think of myself as a doctor actually.'

'Really?'

'Yeah, I mean, I didn't quite graduate high school. But I've seen tons of doctors, and I just feel like I could do it. If they just gave me a shot.'

Violet laughed and stood straight to lean her arm on the wall above the tank. 'Pillow Wilson, Autodidact Doctor. I can see the bus-stop ads in my mind. I'm an advertising expert now.'

'Hey, you learned my last name.'

'You are kind of famous.'

'That is so true. Want to see a kind of famous person's house again?'

Pillow was trying to act and authentically feel less purely horny about this situation than he might have usually. So, he let the old-school sloppy, clothed make-out session on the couch go on for an unduly long time without trying to escalate anything. Violet Hunter had obviously not started out the date thinking of it as a date and probably not wanting it to end by sleeping with him, and he didn't want her to feel like she'd been hustled into anything. They broke for water, and Violet Hunter scooted across the cushion.

She slugged some water and wagged her eyebrows at him. 'All right, all right. Back on topic. Sherlock still hasn't found your car?'

Pillow sat up, graciously tucking his erection into the waistband of his joggers. 'Nope, he's out looking for it now. Seems like if he was going to find it, he'd have found it already.'

'And you don't care?'

Pillow paused for a second, having not really considered it before. 'It's a Bentley, so it is worth more money than I technically have right now, so I should care. But thinking about it with my feelings, nah. It's a car. Who really gives a fuck?'

She stood to get a closer look at the statue. 'You had $8,400 in your pocket the last time I saw you.'

'I wasn't broke the last time I saw you.' He pointed at his cheek. 'This cost me a few bucks. I'll get it back though, after I win.'

'If you're broke, how can you afford this house?'

'Oh, I absolutely can't. Bank takes it if I lose. But when I win, every big name from 147 to 160 pounds is going to be calling me out. I'm seeing three milly, easy. So, I'm not worried about it.'

'What if you lose?'

Pillow shrugged. 'If they rob me on the scorecards, I hide as much liquid cash as I can, declare Chapter 11. From there, we move forward, lay low, take a few small-time fights, have another up-and-comer try me for the name value, beat his ass. One or two decent money fights after that, ride off into the sunset with a small nest egg. Like I said. Easy work.'

'Wow.'

'I'm supposed to be over the hill, right? I've had some shine. I beat a whole run of good fighters, A-level fighters. And I lost when I stepped up to the A+s, the superstar-types. But this kid is supposed to be the real one, the second coming. I beat him now, then this is my run. However many fights I want, pick and choose, mid-seven figures all in a row until I say when.'

Violet Hunter chewed her mildly enflamed lower lip. 'You really live a fucked-up life, Pillow.'

It was occurring to Pillow that he was used to people already being a little bit used to him. He was worried he'd sounded careless. Which he was but didn't want to sound that way. 'It's not that fucked up. I'm an athlete, so mostly I'm just training or chilling at home. Weird camp this time, with the whole Arsène thing. Usually, I keep things low-key.'

Violet Hunter laughed and straightened her shirt a little. 'I think low-key means a different thing to you and me.' She raised her hand to bump the bottom of curls she didn't have yet. 'The guy you're fighting is really good, right? He gets a lot of knockouts.'

'Look at little Miss Boxing Researcher. Yeah, he's really good.'

'Are you scared?'

Pillow made a fist with his right hand and looked at it. Tracing the rivers of tight, scarred-up flesh into his misshapen knuckles. 'Oh, for sure. Yes. Absolutely.'

She shook her head and looked off, above his head.

Pillow was just being himself and that was probably going to make Violet Hunter run away. Because Violet Hunter was a gentle person who felt fine being herself and living her life and not seeing anybody get punched in the face. But this time around, Pillow genuinely was seeing and feeling and acting in the world as if he wasn't first of all horny. Violet Hunter liked him, he knew that, and if she didn't want to be a woman who wanted to fuck a boxer that was fair enough.

'Last time I showed you my shark.' He pointed to the floor-to-ceiling window shitting light freely and loosely through the kitchen into the shark room. 'One more party trick.'

She followed him through the kitchen to the backyard, where Gentleman Jim was lying in a sad little coil. Pillow turned down the Cuban jazz. Violet dropped to her haunches and covered her eyes, then pulled them aside. She left her hands cupped around her eyes like horse blinders, ready to cover them again.

'Giraffes are so cute.' She wasn't crying, but the idea of crying was in her voice. 'She's so young and so sad.' Violet sniffed and stood. She looked up at Pillow but didn't meet his eye. 'I hope you win your fight.' And Pillow felt that familiar sadness of certainty. He watched her smile over her shoulder and do a small wave through the glass of the back door as she left through the wood of the front.

Pillow knew that Violet Hunter was a person who wanted to be with another person, and he wasn't strictly a person these days. He was something people still watched on TV. Pillow walked over to his sleeping animal. He patted Gentleman Jim's flank, then curled in beside her and went to sleep.

On rest days, fighters rest.

Part III

Pillow Fights

I.

Somehow without making itself too obvious, fight week had arrived. Fight week is the week where boxers do their interviews with the media, eat five hundred calories a day, sweat a dozen healthy pound off their bodies, then get weighed to the ounce in front of an audience. It's the week boxers wake up at six in the morning with a pounding headache, eat half an egg's worth of egg white with no salt and drink about a third of the water they need, and then answer diplomatically when asked if they're over their discipline problems.

By the time fight week rolls around, the work is making weight, which this time was only a mild torture to Pillow. Fight week is too late to train, too late to spar. The move is to stay sharp on the pads and do your cardio to get the last few pounds off, but the real work is finished. One day, after he'd gotten in his miles and before a doctor checked to see if he was alive and semicoherent enough to maintain his boxing licence, Pillow was put into a beautiful silk shirt covered in pictures of flowers that looked like thrilled vaginas and told to sit at a long table full of people he hated and answer questions from other people he hated.

Pillow sat at the long table not hearing a thing, only seeing, and only seeing Julio Solis. The Golden Boy, sitting stiff and nervous in his suit. The kid looked, first of all, massive. A good two inches taller than Pillow, and a small ham wider on either side.

Julio Solis had the body of an aircraft carrier and the independent sense of self of also an aircraft carrier. Solis shrinking in his suit as his crazy father ranted and raved and talked all kinds of shit Pillow didn't need to hear to know word for word. Solis finally looked over at Pillow, and the boxer grabbed somebody else's water bottle, took a deep swig, and jogged his eyebrows at the younger man. Solis was looking at Pillow because everyone in the room was looking at Pillow because he'd been asked a question quite a long time ago.

A reporter divorced enough from social reality to be wearing a fedora said: 'Should I repeat … What do you think about Ruben Solis, your opponent's father and manager saying that you're a mobbed-up disgrace to the sport?'

The boxer looked over the heads of all the people for a while. Then, he picked a beautiful woman and spoke to her, because it's easiest to tell your feelings to a beautiful person who is beautiful in a perfectly smooth tiny body and large textured lips sort of way. 'I think that when we're born all we're given is a gorgeous mystery and a little time to be in it and never solve a single thing, and that's all.' He flung a hand that had more metal plates in it than almost any hand in the history of the human animal, and the tips of two of his fingers came to rest awkwardly just below his eye socket.

Nobody said anything, and the boxer leaned back, putting his broken hands as far behind his head as they'd still go. 'That's my opinion on that issue.'

There were a few thousand more words, and then the boxers were supposed to spend a minute or so standing close enough to kiss but not kissing. They did that, and Pillow clasped his hands behind his back, stuck out his chin and placed it above Julio Solis's cocked, quivering fist.

When the two fighters turned to pose for photos, Julio Solis hoisted a huge, gaudy championship belt with every flag in the world on it over his shoulder and past Pillow's face, then held the belt awkwardly in front of his own waist. Pillow nodded, pulled the back off a tiny golden sea-horse belt buckle and stripped the thin, leather belt off his pants, folded it in half, and did the same.

2.

Pillow slept for three hours, then woke from a dream that was just spitting teeth into a hole. Then he ran five miles in twenty-four minutes. He kept walking randomly through the trees, and emerged somehow on a beach, his knees sinking into the wet, receding surface of the sand. When you're spending all your days making your body into an automatic machine that sees another person's eyes and throws a fist between them, you have to let the machine wander for a bit. Follow your automatic body and leave in charge the parts of your computer brain that do all the things that aren't thinking.

The boxer fell gracefully forward, running his flat hands over the tiny bumpy surface of mollusc shells, pressed peanut-butter-cookie deep into the dough of the beach. He picked up a perfect one that was exactly the same as the others and tucked the shell into his eye socket, which was made of seven bones he'd managed not to break yet, and he watched the mollusc, who was mostly a slippery foot, flip its foot of a self loosely back and forth. Pillow pressed the shell gently back into the sand. And the sky was a curtain, he guessed, and it did one of the four things curtains ever do and opened.

The miles were done, but a six-hundred-dollar physiotherapist had told him that miles don't count on sand. The automatic man ran the long way home, and there was nobody looking at him, but he knew that if there had been they'd be asking themselves who can run so softly. Moving back to the streets, Pillow watched the oil of 5 a.m. light flow into the stale standing water of colours in the night, the brick of roofs and the savage separate screams of hanging flowers cutting themselves slowly out of painted walls behind them.

He detoured to another park just to use its footbridge. And each step was a note on a piano that hadn't had a string touched in years, and under a long dark wire that brought light from somewhere else, he crossed a gorge full of the corpses of trees and he tried to breathe the air in deeply, to suck the creosote into his lungs because a twelve-hundred-dollar nutritionist had heard an eighty-dollar naturopath say it's good for the lungs and repeated it to a ten-million-dollar boxer with a twenty-cent right hand. Pillow wondered if birds ever think about anything other than food when they fly.

The boxer went home and weighed himself to the ounce, and the number was good enough for him to drink enough water to not quite soak a face towel and eat enough food to feed a squirrel for half a day. Pillow thought about knowing and things that are over, and how much still happens after you know and after it's over. About things that eat you and the things that eat those things that eat you.

The doorbell rang, and instead of answering the door Pillow threw a grip trainer through his open bedroom window and waited. He listened to Genevieve Hamon drag a six-foot-tall bureau up two storeys one step at a time. In his bedroom, she knocked on the side and all four of the box's wooden sides fell to the floor. On the stand there was a drooping giraffe head and a bright pink gladiator skirt with a picture of a giraffe going to sleep on the waistband. Next to the giraffe gear there was a terry cloth robe dyed to a slightly more boring than tea towel grey.

Genevieve wasn't the sort of person to talk when a wag of the eyebrows would do.

Pillow got up and looked at each item in turn. He took the gladiator skirt and the terry cloth robe. He held the skirt in his hands and closed his eyes. What was either Genevieve Hamon or a sea anemone fixed his lip with a kiss that was moist around the edges and full of tiny, dry grips in the middle. And then he opened his eyes and Genevieve Hamon's mouth was as big and wet as a sea and it said: 'There's really no difference between plants and animals and rocks, is there, Pillow?'

Pillow thought about water and wetness and how we all die all alone. 'I don't know the full deal on plants or rocks or animals. I'm sure I asked for this giraffe head thing at some point.'

The boxer smiled, reached into the pocket of his joggers, and threw her a brick of cash he didn't have.

Pillow spent the rest of the night inspecting his entire torso with a large and small mirror, plucking stray hairs. He weighed himself again, grimaced, and drank enough water to make a short espresso, ate enough chickpeas to feed a baby hamster for two weeks, and then sat in his backyard wearing a beautifully stitched giraffe head, watching Gentleman Jim listlessly shuffle in perfect anti-rhythm to Cuban jazz.

Giraffes probably don't think perfectly stitched fake giraffe heads are anything in particular. They just know they're not fruit or a dominant male or an infinite pasture to graze through until they die.

3.

Public workouts are a half-hour when, as you're cutting weight and preparing to strip to the waist and fight another grown man in front of a few thousand people for money, a bunch of photographers take pictures of you as you work out. You spend your life in the gym working hard, and then you play-act working hard for a few minutes. Most of the time, boxers get in there, do some calisthenics they might have done anyway, get a little stretch on, and then do a pre-choreographed pad routine that looks impressive and means less than nothing. Sometimes, the foreign guys will do a little dance routine from their culture, which Pillow always liked.

You get one body, and the only thing you really get to do with it is all the things you have to do to keep your brain wanting to be alive. So, with everybody expecting him to do the public workout bit, the least taxing training that looks the best, Pillow went out and did a real one. He walked onto the mats and did thirteen consecutive minutes of high knees, then he made his body into a small shallow boat, punching himself as hard as he could in the stomach until Kim told him to stop.

He stood and a bunch of microphones surrounded him, and Pillow shouted at everyone rather than taking questions from anyone. 'See, this motherfucker Solis, he's on that apex predator shit. He's got the thumbs. He's got the brains. He's people. Me, little old me, I'm the wide open sea. I've been around a lot longer, and kids like this rode on me in little boats to other parts of the world to kill every single person they met, and all that. This motherfucker Solis, Mr. Whole-Ass Human Species, he's dumping poison into me and the sky overtop of me and he's boiling me slowly year by year. It's already happened. Right? I'm the ocean. And, I'll be around awhile longer, but I'm also dead already, really.

But here's the thing about people and the ocean. People won, I guess. They used the ocean and got a lot out of it and they dumped all their garbage into it and the ocean had no choice but to take it. But the ocean can take it. And one day soon, it'll swell up and suck people all the way out into itself where they can't breathe. And everyone'll be begging the ocean to stop and they're so used to getting what they ask for that they won't realize the ocean just does what the ocean does. It's not what anyone asked or paid for: it's the motherfucking truth. And it was here before us, and it'll kill us all and stick around after. That's your fight preview.'

The room was silent, and in a lot of other places the ocean was very loud.

Pillow left to go sit in a quiet room by himself, not eating.

4.

Pillow woke up from a mild starvation nap to find a septuagenarian mob boss in his living room polishing a raven's belly. It was impossible to tell if the white strip of fabric wrapped around Gwynn Apollinaire's head was a scarf or a bandage. It was too hot outside for a scarf and too loose around her head for a bandage. The two faceless men in black suits tracked him with the emptiness of their gun barrels. She held the raven away from herself and looked at the buffed surface of its metal tummy, then she took a pair of tweezers and used them to move a tiny, bird-sized cigarette from her pocket into the sculpture's mouth.

'Say, Pillow, I've got a brainteaser for you.'

'Sure.'

'What is the least amount of money you'd have to be paid to make love with a male ape?'

'I'm not sure that's a brainteaser, Gwynn.'

'You have a clear and definite answer?'

'No.'

'Consider your brain teased, my sweet. Teasing is the only thing in the world that's actually good for you.' She put the raven down on his coffee table. 'I'm not sure you're aware of how few people in my position in life, a mob boss of some small esteem, would come to someone who chose to occupy your position in life, that of a slash-faced man fighting as an already dire underdog, bearing the gift of this beautiful raven statue, rather than another species of gift. A whole other species.'

Pillow accepted the statue. It was a nice one, but Pillow couldn't help thinking it would look better if it were breathing real air instead of pretending to smoke. 'Listen, it's all still good. One more day, then it's done.'

Apollinaire flopped back on the couch, looking like a painting of a fainting woman someone did to make fun of some slightly older paintings of fainting women. 'To quote the man with whom I speak: "Bet everything that's not tied down." Really, it was a very stylish thing to say, and as the stylish always does, it left us with a question.' It didn't particularly seem like the faceless men breathed or moved the way living flesh moves, but their guns made the ambient sounds metal makes when you hold it as still as you can while you're thinking about killing someone kind of famous. 'What's tied down?'

'Didn't we already do this? With the baby and all.'

She levitated back to a seated position like a mummy coming out of a crypt because a whole swarm of scarabs told her to. 'I like a little follow-up. To drive things home.'

Pillow's hand cramped completely, curling into a thin, desiccated claw. A hand that had used to belong to a witch and now belonged to her melted corpse. 'Drive whatever you want wherever you want it. I'm still going to win.'

Apollinaire nodded. 'Do you ever feel like the bush of your body has had all the roses picked?'

'Absolutely. Yes.'

Gwynn sprang to her feet and, as if tied to some kind of reverse pulley, the gun barrels dropped at the same time and the faceless men moved into the empty space of the hallway. She clapped him on both shoulders and went straight in for it. Pillow liked kissing in general, so he let the makeout go on, super wetly and completely sexlessly for a while you could have described as long if you were feeling dramatic about it.

Gwynn dropped back onto her heels and punched him as hard as she could, and Pillow's abdomen took the full force without caring or knowing that caring is a thing other parts of your body do about punches. 'Business. You say you're going to win.'

'For sure.'

'Good, because the odds have continued to pile up against you. We're getting eleven to one now.'

'Bet it all. Everything that's not tied down.'

Gwynn cocked her head and looked behind her, as if surprised. 'And what's that? A wind from the south, and one by one each of the pomegranate blossoms of our hearts are loosed from the trembling branch of this world into the empty, dying stream of chance. Which is to say, I'm doubling down, and I would appreciate if you'd do the same.'

'I still don't have the cash for that.'

'So, we'll keep doing it then.'

'What?'

'Whatever the hell it is we've been doing all along.'

Gwynn clasped her hands loosely, wrapping four fingers around the stem of her thumb, looking like the exact opposite of a person who has ever been startled by a breeze.

5.

After a sleep that felt more like a tiny death, Pillow met Kim at his sauna, stripped naked and allowed her to oil his entire skin. He was coming in light for this fight, but he still had six pounds to sweat off. Twenty-five minutes later he stepped out of the sauna, and Kim scraped the sweat off his body with a credit card, weighed him, grimaced. 'I need another pound from you.'

Pillow had staggered to sit on the ground. He let his head loll comfortably to the side. 'Kim, do you ever dream that one day we won't need these skin husks anymore? And we can all just sleep and postfuck in a giant soup together? Drain every bit of ourselves out and pour it into something that actually fucking matters at all? Do you dream that?' He wasn't sure when he'd started crying because he was so dehydrated he only got a few tears out. He felt he was crying by the swell behind his eyes. 'It's what I wanted since I was a little kid. I wanted it so bad. And I got all of it. And I was such a sad little kid. Does it have to hurt so much and every time and more every time?' He banged his tin can head against the tile.

Kim nodded neutrally, bent over, and scraped a saltless tear off his cheek with the credit card. 'Tears are water weight, end of the day. We still need the pound, Pete.'

Pillow knocked on his head as if he were picking his brain up for prom, then he stuck the hand out and Kim pulled him to stand.

Looking a lot more like a version of himself that had been rescued after sixty days at sea clinging to a buoy than anyone really wants him to look, Pillow staggered to the scale wrapped in a towel and closed his eyes as a few men weighed him, and then they announced the weight and some people clapped and he stepped off the scale.

Julio Solis looked a lot more like a giant airship waiting patiently to be filled up before it floats to Belgium than anyone who had to fight him the next day would really want him to look. The young fighter walked calmly onto the scale, flexed, and morphed briefly into what a werewolf would look like if full moons happened often enough to allow for a consistent twelve-week bodybuilding program, and then smiled for the camera as his weight was announced as the exact number it was supposed to be. Solis stepped off the scale grinning, took a small sip of electrolyte water, and gained sixteen healthy pounds. The two boxers faced off, breathed hunger-strike breath in each other's faces, then put on their joggers and left through different doors.

Returning home, Pillow sat on the edge of his bed and drank seven bottles of water using a bottlecap as a cup and watched two birds raze a giant dog's back and then sow the raw patch with seeds, and then he watched a row of eggplants grow as the dog desperately tried to win six dog races and lost each one. It was probably a cartoon.

6.

Pillow supposed that he'd been talking about dying too much and it was making Kim and Painlevé uncomfortable, so he decided to think about dying quietly to himself instead. Painlevé, decked out in his cutman gear, was wrapping Pillow's hands with gauze, and there were twelve people watching him do it. One of the twelve people initialled the wraps, and then another of the twelve people followed him into the bathroom and watched the boxer pee in a cup, and then took the cup. The commission guy walked away holding Pillow's pee, and then Pillow retrieved the gelcap amphetamines Sherlock had prepared from where he'd stashed them in the garbage and dry swallowed all of them at once.

Kim slid the shiny, six-shades-of-pink gloves over Pillow's hands. He punched the wall to break them in, then hit mitts, stretched, cried in the corner with a towel over his head. As he sat staring into the diamond of ground between his legs and breathing, Kim sat down beside him. She slipped an arm over his shoulder and spoke directly into his ear. 'You're my special flower, Pillow. And I know it's hard. The real work isn't gardening, it's growing. You're my special flower and you don't owe me shit. You were born ready, and then we got you readier just in case.' The boxer tipped his head onto the rigid mass ball of her shoulder and nodded at something that was true.

They called him for the prefight interview. Pillow reminded himself not to talk too directly about dying. It was probably okay to say he was willing to die but hoped he wouldn't and that, if he did, dying was something that didn't remind you of being alive and that you couldn't imagine while you were alive. That dying was to the living what air conditioning is to a sea anemone. But there probably wasn't any need to go into that kind of detail and he didn't think people would understand what he meant by it.

It was an old man in a suit whose voice was a perfectly tuned radio. 'How are you feeling tonight, Pillow?'

'Perfect, I'm going to win instead of dying.'

The radio said 'ha' once. 'So, that's settled. What's next then? What are you looking to do after this fight?'

Pillow used the heel of his glove to rub the thin, perfectly smooth skin of the radio's face. 'Great question. I've got a lot of goals for the future, a lot of things I'd like to do. Long term, I'd really like to sublimate into a gas.'

'Could … could you say more about that?'

'So, in this situation where I've become a gas, it's like I'm floating in the room, and you're breathing me, but I am also there and knowing everything and present in a *where's Pillow?*, *oh wait, he's there as a cloud* sort of way. That's … I mean it'll be a lot of work, and a lot would have to change and develop to make that into a possibility, but I would love to make that move after this fight if I could.'

'The transition into an omniscient gas?'

'Yeah, that's right.' Pillow did a long, evocative shimmy with his shoulders, cupped the elderly radio's genitals with his glove and hoisted them slightly before sliding back into his own personal space. 'I've been solid so long. Let's switch it up. I've done just about everything you can do to get to know someone with your body. I want to know what it would be like to be breathed in and out by someone I love. Let's try that one on. See how it goes.'

The old-timey radio coughed twice dryly through the wrought metal gate of his teeth. 'I think that's our time.'

'Great.' Pillow skipped away whistling the sort of song a very old cartoon hobo carrying a very old cartoon bindle whistles after he's stolen a very old cartoon pie.

By the time he had to walk out, Pillow felt luminous and beautiful and a little bit afraid of having a stroke. Pillow put his gloved hands on Kim's shoulders and started following her down the tunnel. The tunnel narrowed as they got closer to the light and the noise of the crowd. Pillow's mouth was completely dry, and his skin was being painted on with a brush dipped in light.

Pillow hit the end of the tunnel, and he couldn't hold Kim anymore. He felt his gloves slip off her shoulders as he slid across the threshold, already dancing. He danced all the way to the ring, considered a flip over the top rope, and then remembered abstractly that he was about to fight for twelve rounds. He waited for Kim to step on the rope to let him walk through.

The two fighters met at centre ring and a referee said rules at them. Pillow looked Julio Solis in the eyes and Solis held the stare, seeming about as scared as a vulture is of a dead dog. They touched gloves and went back to their corners. Kim fed a piece of plastic with lion's teeth painted on it into Pillow's mouth. She kissed him on the neck and then it was just Pillow and an old man and a huge, happy boy floating in a vast, lonesome ocean of canvas together.

Pillow came out on his toes with his eyes unnaturally wide, moving laterally and looking to get a read on Solis's movement. He flashed some jabs and started working his feints. The kid stalked him at a moderate pace, underreacting, cutting Pillow off and catching punches on his forearms. Seeing an opening, Pillow tapped a hot-stove jab off Solis's forehead, then sunk a stiff body jab into the pit of the young fighter's stomach. Pillow hit a quick pivot, ducked Solis's counter, and ripped off a double left hook, catching the kid flush on the cheek with the second shot. Having done the only clean work of the round, Pillow circled behind his jab, trying to keep Julio chasing while killing the rest of the time. It was a boring round for the crowd and a perfect round for Pillow, who was now seeing the younger fighter squaring up, frustrated with the footwork.

Pillow went back to the corner and took his drink of water and spit it out, ignoring Kim as she gave him instructions. He looked past her shoulder at Julio Solis, watching the young boxer sit there with his legs stretched out, brow furrowed as his father screamed at him. Pillow didn't feel sorry for the kid or himself or anything in the world.

The next round started the same way, Solis following instead of cutting Pillow off, eating snappy jabs to the face and the odd spear to the sternum. Pillow heard Kim shout from the corner thirty seconds in, catching Julio's reaching jab and digging a shovel hook to the ribs on the return, and then he woke up when his forehead hit the canvas and enough of his blood to paint a small flowerpot fell to the canvas next to his eye in one blunt splatter, like someone had squashed a Ziploc bag.

Pillow was, if nothing else at all in the world at this moment, a veteran fighter. So, he knew to take a knee and find the ref for the count. He was surprised to see the arterial old man flashing seven fingers already, and he waited another second before driving up, hoping his legs would hold. They quasi-did and the ref wondered with a scream if he was okay. Pillow cocked his head as if somebody had very mildly cut him off in traffic, nodded loosely, and said, 'All day.' And the ref wiped imaginary dust off his gloves and cleared out of the way to let Julio Solis knock him unconscious. Pillow's legs were good to stand but still didn't quite have a good enough grasp of Earth's gravity to move him around reliably, so the old boxer sagged back into the ropes and waited. Solis rushed in and launched wide hooks, trying to get the ref to step in more than to knock Pillow out. It was an easy mistake to make, but a big one. Pillow rolled with the shots, finally weaving under a hook and digging a hard left hook of his own to Solis's solar plexus as the bell sounded and the ref pulled them apart. Pillow blew Julio Solis a gloved kiss.

The old boxer staggered back to his corner, where Kim caught him under the arms and settled him onto the stool. She took a deep breath in through her nose and out through her mouth and Pillow copied her. Painlevé went to work on Pillow's gash, which had spent six weeks healing and the smallest possible unit of a second opening back up to slightly wider than it had ever been. Pillow moved instinctively to touch the cut with his glove and Kim clamped down on his hand, sticking her eyes close enough to his that he had to look in them.

Pillow said what he felt in his heart. 'Owww.'

'Okay, listen: that was your round until he caught you.'

'What'd he get me with?'

'Overhand right over your left hook.'

'Shit.'

'Hey, so don't do that again? Right. Stay sharp, and if you dig those counters to the body, this bitch is going to break down. He went and blew half his wad already trying to finish you. Just make sure you bring your feet with you. Quick shots inside, then back on the bike.'

'Easy work.' Pillow winked the eye that didn't have blood spouting out from under it.

Painlevé finished sprinkling caustic powder into Pillow's wound and smeared a thick layer of Vaseline overtop. The little Frenchman pulled back and admired his work, kissing the tips of his gloved fingers, then spit out a little Vaseline and rubbed the rest over his lips.

Kim moved an ice bag over Pillow's chest. 'He thinks you want to brawl him, so he's ready to get boxed up. All you, baby. Slip, slide, keep turning him, keep up that stick. Float like a butterfly … '

Pillow took a beautiful breath through his nose. 'And fuck every bee.'

Kim grabbed him behind the head and looked into his eyes. 'That's what the queen does. You my queen bee, Pillow. You the queen bee, now get out there … ' Pillow stood and the stool disappeared from under him. 'Get that train run on you, boy. Queen bee gets dick for days.'

Huge men in little-boy blazers were pulling Kim out of the ring. Pillow looked out at the crowd and smiled kindly at no one in particular.

For just a little while more, Pillow's legs were two long bamboo poles carrying the weight of a full-grown man. He tried to move around the ring, and Solis caught him almost immediately with a left hook. Pillow's knees gave out. He found his balance and immediately folded his arms at the elbow and did an exaggerated chicken dance to play it off.

It did not quite work.

The young fighter calmly dug hurtful body shots, shouldering Pillow into the corner and keeping the inside position, shrugging off the older fighter's weak attempts to clinch. Pillow grabbed a collar tie and looked to the ref just in time to see Julio's looping left hook come over the top and smash the gob of Vaseline that had been keeping his cut closed; it flew through the air over the crowd. Julio ducked in low and rocked Pillow with a head-butt, digging in with a withering right hook to the ribs behind it.

Pillow finally got the purchase on an underhook and dug in, turning the bigger man back into the corner. He reached over for the full hug. At some point he'd bloodied Solis's nose and there was an adorable little dollop of blood on the kid's shoulder. Pillow leaned in and kissed the dollop. The kid tasted hydrated. Solis yelled out and the ref reached in to break them up, and Pillow sucked wind and blood until the ref finally managed to pry them apart, waving his fingers in Pillow's face.

'Don't bite him!'

'I was kissing.'

'What?'

'My heart is full. Fuck. I'm … my heart is full.'

'Quit it or it's a point.'

'Why?'

'Don't argue with me.'

'I'm asking.'

'Last warning.'

As he stumbled back into the opposite turnbuckle, Pillow knew it doesn't help much to think about points when the guy you're fighting is coming for your soul. He ate four vicious hooks to the head before he caught Solis in another clinch. The ref pried them apart.

Another finger in the face. 'No holding.'

'It's love.'

The ref's eyes bulged out like they'd just had stents put in, and his face turned a shade of red that made clear those stents were best used elsewhere. 'TIME!' He grabbed Pillow's glove and turned him to each judge. 'That's a point. That's a point. That's a point. One point, holding.' He wagged his finger one more time in Pillow's face and restarted the clock.

If the ref had really wanted to punish Pillow, he could have just let Solis keep punching him, but instead he'd fallen for the trick and given Pillow time to recover. Pillow's legs were now very long bamboo sticks with a nice layer of varnish over them. They did still have to carry a full-grown man's weight, though.

Solis hit him flush with a 3–2–3 combination, rocking his head from side to side with each punch. Pillow managed to get the outside foot position and escaped to centre ring. Julio chased him a little eagerly, and Pillow sunk in a hard jab to the stomach before getting cornered again and weathering another savage beating. He heard the ten-second clapper and ducked into Solis, blindly trading hooks and getting a few solid body shots in before Solis caught him with an equatorial left hook and staggered him as the bell rang. The air was full of thick jelly, but all the old boxer did was shrug and purse his lips slightly, as if being told his order would be another minute or two at a food truck.

A cold, wet sponge hit him in the face and hands pushed him onto the stool.

'It's in the mouthguard.'

Kim pulled the mouthguard out. Pillow's tooth and a shot glass full of his blood tipped into her hand.

Pillow spit up some blood on the flappy pink tassels of his gladiator skirt. 'Hits like a bitch. Eating a lace curtain's pussy, what it feels like.'

Kim passed the tooth past the head it had come from, then settled into Pillow's face, holding out a steady finger. 'Breathe.'

Talking is worse than breathing. Pillow stayed quiet. He had some more unfocused sexual thoughts about upholstery.

Kim stuck the ice bag behind his head. 'Let me put some water on your balls.'

Talking was still a bad idea, and he couldn't nod his head without maybe getting some of Painlevé's intensely caustic coagulant powder in his eye, so he stayed still and waited for the ice water to hit. Nobody in the history of the world as beat up as Pillow has ever turned down having ice water poured on their balls.

'Pillow, man, you gotta show me something here.'

Talking is one of the worst things, really. But sometimes you need to do it to stop people from doing things that will bankrupt you and ruin your life. 'Don't.'

'Then show me something. I can't let you be a punching bag.'

'I'm breaking him down. He don't have it.'

'You're not breaking down shit. Box. Move, no more ropes, no more trading hooks. Box and move or the towel's coming in.'

The attendants pulled Kim away, and Pillow was back in the middle of the wide open sea of a fight he was losing by four points, a tooth, twenty pounds, a pint of blood, and three concussions. Six ice cubes fell out of his skirt.

The fourth round went less horrifically for Pillow. He had his legs back under him and kept Julio Solis off him with slick footwork and a couple clean check hooks. Solis was warmed up now, and he did catch Pillow in the corner a couple times, snapping the older fighter's head back with clean right hands. Pillow was taking the shots better now, seeing them coming, rolling with the hooks. He lost the round and took another beating but didn't get hurt. The bell rang and he did a cute shuffle and patted Julio Solis on the butt.

Everybody had calmed down a bit in his corner. Nothing had landed on the cut and the coagulant was starting to work. Kim rewarded Pillow with a long drink and patted him on the jaw.

'You got your sea legs now. One more round like that and we can start walking him down, all right? He's losing steam and this kid can't fight backing up.'

Pillow peeked over her shoulder and looked at Solis, his father still yelling, the kid's chin drooped down between his collarbones, abs heaving. 'Sea legs ain't shit. Gills, motherfucker. Glug glug.'

Kim slapped him hard on the stomach. 'Pete. Listen, keep moving one more round. He ain't getting no second wind. Stay crispy and you'll get him down the stretch.'

Pillow blinked twice dreamily and smiled. 'Gills. Fish lung all day. Fish lung.'

Waiting for the ref to start the time, Pillow looked at Julio Solis, standing with his weight in his heels, waiting for the round to start. Pillow had been coming out for the rounds in a loose, relaxed posture. He'd lope out the first few steps, then drop into his proper stance and start fighting. This time, he took two careless steps forward, then, hearing the bell, sprinted across the ring and caught Solis cold with a leaping left hook. Pillow turned to his corner and pointed his round cartoon hand at Kim. It was a flash knockdown, Solis wasn't hurt at all, just surprised and off-balance. Pillow skipped around in the corner mugging to the crowd, and, once Solis was back up, he took the rest of the round off, moving laterally and clowning. Solis chased him gamely and caught him with a couple body shots, but didn't expend too much energy either, knowing he couldn't make up the knockdown. The kid was learning.

In the corner, Kim kissed him softly on the head. 'You're such a fuckin' cutie-pie. Listen: we got two rounds with a knockdown, he's got three rounds with a knockdown and the point. Stay relaxed, let's keep boxing. He is more tired than you.'

Pillow wondered how soon after it leaves water a fish knows it's going to die. Does it ever figure it out? Or does it just happen? He imagined a knife going through the vent of his shark's lungs. Painlevé poured more chemicals into the hole in his face and sealed them in with jelly. The bell rang again, which meant he had to keep fighting someone with only his sad, orphan hands.

They came out for another low-action round that Pillow knew he was winning and knew just as certainly the judges wouldn't give him. He kept up with the body shots and was starting to see just the slightest sag in Solis's tight, muscled-up body. Looking like a flag with just enough wind under it to remind you that all countries are is a reason it's okay for some people to starve to death and other people to die of eating too much candy. Julio Solis swung a right hook hard enough to chop down a very small tree, and Pillow tilted his hip a fraction of an inch and let it glance off his shoulder. Solis stumbled and caught himself, bouncing to regather.

At the end of the round, Pillow dug in for a flurry inside and, suddenly realizing he was completely gassed, backed off into the corner. Solis chased him down and threw everything he had into a sweeping right to the body. Pillow skipped to the side and pulled his waist back, the punch sailing wide. Pillow stopped moving, held his glove over his eye and looked out into the crowd, watching the fiction of the punch sail over the crowd. The bell rang. A nice thing about boxing is that they hit a real bell with a hammer.

Kim rubbed some blood back into his arm and whispered in his ear. 'You're styling on him now, baby. He's biting on the half-step feint all night. Okay, half-step, pop the shoulder, he's got nothing. Pet, pet, slap, let's do it.'

Pillow was right that second exclusively in the business of reading and reacting. It was a good sign that she wasn't soothing him anymore, just giving him actual boxing advice. Was he winning? What would a dog act like if you put a groundhog's brain in it? What building was he in again? If a groundhog sees another groundhog get hit by a car, do they realize the other groundhog is dead? What city?

Pillow was tired and deeply neurologically hurt, but he felt good. He had his range and his reads, and Solis was only having more trouble timing him as the fight went on. Pillow gazed over at the younger man and noted the red welting lining the kid's rib cage. The old boxer had gassed his arms out so badly that they had pins and needles now.

The Golden Boy came on strong, with hard, technical punches, but he was too slow, too rote. Pillow kept freezing the kid with feints, scoring with flicking jabs and soft, darting right hands on the outside. When Solis finally got close enough to throw his right hand, Pillow hit a slick slip pivot, turned him into the corner, and ripped two hooks to the body, feinted, then shrugged and waltzed back to centre ring, motioning for his opponent to follow.

Pillow had been waiting for Solis to drop his elbows to stop the body shots up the middle. The old boxer banged a jab into Julio's guard just to be sure, and then he dropped his level again, feinting the body shot and coming upstairs with an overhand right. In the last thirty seconds of the round, Pillow threw more overhand rights than he had in the last seven years. What had been a little scratch on Solis's eyebrow bloomed into a gash, some swelling immediately pushing into the kid's eye.

Pillow sat down smiling and then Kim's face was the entire visible universe. 'I don't need you out there sprinkling pixie dust like you a creature of the fuckin' forest, all right? Get out there and beat this motherfucker's ass. No tinkerbell bullshit. Slice this motherfucker's eyeball with a razor blade. Stuff this motherfucker's carcass in a piano, play a little tune, and then drag his ass across a deserted country field. GET ME THE GOLDEN BOY'S FUCKIN' EYE!' She turned around and shouted toward Solis, who couldn't possibly have heard. 'GOLDEN EYEBALL, NOM NOM NOM!'

Solis came out hard for the next round. Pillow managed to spin him into the corner, and instead of punching waltzed back to centre ring and waited. When Solis didn't follow him right away, Pillow grinned and curtsied. Pillow saw Solis take a deep breath through his nose and bear down. And he knew the kid wanted to do something, make an impact, and he knew it was time to do the cakewalk. The old boxer tossed out an up-jab and L-stepped out, then strolled toward the corner, crossing his feet. And Julio, grunting for breath, his eye swelling, saw Pillow's feet cross and lunged into a big, slow right hand; Pillow rolled and threw his right over the top. It was the perfect shot, the one-hitter quitter. Pillow didn't even feel it; he saw it from behind, the clean right hand power shot landing square on Solis's cut. He landed the shot every fighter dreams of, and, because of any boxer he could have possibly been he was Pillow Fist Pete Wilson, the punch didn't knock Solis out cold or even drop him. Rather the Golden Boy staggered back two small steps, touched his eye with his glove, and waded forward. Meanwhile, several bones in Pillow's hand had moved several millimetres away from where they were supposed to be. A distance that's unimportant anywhere but inside your body. He felt the familiar stab go all the way from the tips of his fingers to his shoulder and felt the hot swelling starting immediately.

Solis lunged forward and Pillow stuck him with a hard jab to the belly and slapped the kid on the eye with a check left hook, slipped two slow punches, and sat down on a body shot. The bell rang and Solis walked back to his corner shaking his head. Pillow got up on his tiptoes and theatrically slunk back to his corner like a cat stealing cheese in a black-and-white cartoon.

Pillow got back to the corner, and he and Kim stared into each other's eyes and, in perfect time with each other, took two deep breaths. He didn't consider telling her his hand was broken. Pillow tipped his head down, spit his mouthpiece and as much blood as flows through an adult male's foot in an afternoon into her hand. Kim grabbed his head and squirted some water in his mouth. 'Don't swallow, rinse. Beautiful boxing. All day, you've taken his heart, now you gotta take his soul. Take his whole fuckin' essence.'

Pillow peeked past her shoulder and saw Solis's legs stretched all the way out on his stool. He wondered if any of either of their kidneys still worked.

The officials started getting everyone out. Pillow stood and the stool disappeared from under him. He opened wide and Kim put his mouthpiece in. 'You took the starch out of him with the body work, but don't forget that eye. Hunt that fuckin' eye.' The official grabbed her shoulder, and Kim took one step through the ropes, and turned. 'And Pillow ... '

'Yeah?'

'Fuck the moon.'

Pillow knew what he needed to do. He hurried to centre ring, pushing the ref's arm away, getting a warning and not caring. The round started and Pillow walked straight to Solis with his hands down. He slipped two slow punches and ripped a double left hook, sending Solis staggering back. He followed, hands raised above his head.

'Grateful?'

Half-step feint, open-handed slap with the left hook.

'Grateful, Julio? You feeling grateful now?'

Solis lunged on a hook and Pillow ripped a right uppercut to the gut, almost taking a knee from the pain. Julio tried for some get-back and Pillow cut a sharp angle and sent the kid off-balance into the ropes. The old boxer stood perfectly still in the middle of the ring until Julio finally lurched into Pillow's power jab. The kid winced and stumbled backwards. Pillow stepped in hard for two tapping jabs, pendulum-stepped back, and smashed an over-hand right into the swollen eye. Solis couldn't see the shots coming. Pillow shook the right hand out and stepped forward into a six-punch flurry before the ref, arms waving, bumped him aside. Pillow fell flat into the sea of the canvas and looked up at the sky, which was also the ref hugging Solis with one arm and waving the other in the air, stopping the fight.

Then, the world was a happy scream and a whole lot of bang-ing on his arms and head for a long time. Pillow got pushed in a few directions, and then decided to sit down to see if that made everyone leave him alone, and it did. Kim picked him up and carried him to each corner of the ring, and then she put him down about a foot away from Julio Solis. The two men hugged and Pillow kissed the kid's neck sloppily. Solis grabbed Pillow's wrist and lifted his hand in the air, and someone dropped a heavy, gaudy championship belt with every country in the world's flag on the old boxer's shoulder.

Julio in his ear. 'You're the real shit. You're real.'

'You too. Everything they say, kid. You'll get it. It's coming.'

Solis grinned. 'Rematch? You'll give me the rematch?'

Pillow laughed and tapped the kid on a pec that was also an ancient home carved into the side of a mountain. 'No fuckin' way. Shit's gone real wrong for me if I'm fighting you again.' And the two boxers laughed at something that was true. 'I'll love you forever, Julio.'

'You too, brother. Forever.'

Pillow staggered a few feet away. Kim caught him under the arms and settled him back on his stool. The boxer smiled, kissed each member of his corner on the mouth, and then showed his first outward signs of fatigue in the whole fight, dropping to his knees and puking blood into a bucket for quite a long time.

7.

The only person Pillow let ride in the ambulance was Kim, who held the hand that wasn't broken.

'You really fucking did it. You showed 'em.'

Pillow grinned semi-toothlessly. 'Never in doubt.'

Kim flipped her braids and laughed again. 'Fuck them, actually. You did you. That was you out there, and it's something beautiful. Something beautiful that can take a beating.'

Pillow rinsed and suctioned his mouth. 'I'm talented as fuck, I look good. A lot of ways, I'm the shit. But there's a big important difference between feeling confident and feeling like you're worth shit.'

She patted him on the hand. 'I know.'

'This hand is always going to break.'

'I know that too.' Kim squeezed the hand that was still a unified part of his body. 'You're the one for me, Pillow. Ride or die.'

'Or both.'

'And both, all day.'

They rode the rest of the way to the hospital hand in hand in silence. Once they got there, a group of people in masks spent three hours screwing one of Pillow's bones back to itself in three places, which is something that sounds impossible but happens to someone somewhere every day.

Pillow had a party in his hospital bed for three days. A giant bulging envelope full of a stupid amount of money came by way of a horny septuagenarian mob boss. Two scientists let him cuddle with a tamed vampire bat for a while and assured him that they'd find a great home for the giraffe and the shark soon. A lovely woman with a cute tiny head sent him a bunch of wildflowers with a business card for a tutoring company attached. A loose piece of shit in a coat that was also an entire polar bear came by with a list of names and numbers for his next fight to look over. There weren't any detectives. He wondered how long Violet Hunter's hair had gotten by now.

Eventually a car moved underneath and around him until he was home standing in the middle of a giant ceramic pillow that must have been a joke at some point. He went inside and sat with his shark for a while and hugged his title belt as he watched a video feed of the sloth that had been sad as his pet painfully slowly and joyfully crawl across a very short pipe pretending to be a branch. He watched Jersey Joe nuzzle hopefully into it, still dumb enough to hope that a pipe could be a tree and a pear would fall off.

The door opened and closed and Sherlock Holmes stayed standing. 'Pillow, I've something to show you.'

It had gotten dark at some point, and Pillow was staring at his dark green car on the white ceramic pillow, doing what cars do when they're alone. Which is not much.

'You are one fuck of a detective.'

'And you, dear Pillow, are one fuck of a boxer.'

The two men laughed and retired to the backyard to watch Gentleman Jim settle in for bedtime. Pillow rubbed his giant cartoon hand against the side of his always scarring head. 'Lupin didn't have anything to do with it, right?'

Holmes pulled out his pipe. 'I've a feeling you may have solved this mystery long before I did, but as you are the client and I the hired hand, I'll humour you nonetheless.' He took one empty hit off the pipe, then returned it to the infinity of his pockets. 'Does Blood of the Poet Health and Human Optimization sound familiar to you?'

The boxer grimaced and looked down at his giant, puffy hand. 'Vaguely.'

'The car was there. Where they say you left it and bought a statue several weeks ago. For which you left a $3,000 deposit and never returned. Do you remember doing that?'

Pillow smiled and spent a comfortable while moving his tongue between his gold tooth and the empty space where the next one would be. 'If they say I did, I'd believe it. I lose time.'

Sherlock patted him dryly on the shoulder. Gentleman Jim coiled into a sad, restful lump to sleep.

Pillow leaned his rusty old head to rest on Sherlock's shoulder. 'Boxers say the hardest thing is that you know it's going to end. That you've got this tiny, tiny window that'll maybe never open. If it ever does open it'll be just long enough for you to peek in and then it'll slam shut and break your spine. But I think maybe that's the good part. That this shit ends and I don't. If I'm really trying to really be good, I think maybe the end will be my chance to see. To see who else I can be. We'll find out, I guess.' Pillow straightened up and winked the rest of his swollen eye. 'Or is this one of those times where you've already figured it out, Sherlock? You got there immediately and the whole thing's the rest of us finally meeting you there?'

Sherlock patted him on the back and rubbed the ribs right behind his heart. 'I can only say and only know that the air of this world is sweeter for your presence, Pillow.'

Pillow laughed, adjusted the giant gold-plated belt with every flag in the world on his shoulder, and looked back to the dark yard. Gentleman Jim's head sprang up from her flank, turning to the side as if dodging a dead tree. The neck stilled itself, pausing aimlessly before coiling to rest on the pillow of her body.

Notes

p. 41 – 'One time … ' is paraphrased from Guillaume Apollinaire's 'La jolie rousse' from *Calligrammes: Poèmes de la paix et de la guerre 1913–1916* (1918).

p. 43 – 'The other day … ' is paraphrased from Guillaume Apollinaire's 'L'océan de terre' from *Calligrammes: Poèmes de la paix et de la guerre 1913–1916* (1918).

p. 57 – The character of Violet Hunter and most of the details of her adventure are adapted from Sir Arthur Conan Doyle's 'The Adventure of the Copper Beaches' (1892).

p. 84 – 'It's easy enough … ' is paraphrased from Jean Painlevé's *De la similtude des longueurs et des vitesses* (1937).

p. 85 – 'Painlevé's point was … ' is paraphrased from Jean Painlevé's 'Mystères et miracles de la nature' originally published in *VU*, 29 March, 1931.

p. 121 – '… curved three-pound metal … ' is based on a description of Alberto Giacometti's sculpture *The Palace at 4 a.m* (1932).

p. 158 – 'But Julio Solis, the Golden Boy … ' is paraphrased (quite directly) from Arthur Cravan, included in *4 Dada Suicides: selected texts of Arthur Cravan, Jacques Rigaut, Julien Torma, Jacques Vaché* (2005); actual quote is from, like, 1915.

p. 161 – 'To stand, feet in the water … ' is paraphrased from Jean Painlevé's 'Les pieds dans l'eau,' first published in *Voilà*, 4 May 1935.

p. 173 – 'And love … ' is paraphrased from Guillaume Apollinaire's 'Le pont Mirabeau,' from *Alcools* (1913).

p. 184 – 'Time … ' is from Maurice Leblanc's *The Extraordinary Adventures of Arsène Lupin* (1907).

p. 188 – 'Science is fiction' is generally a thing Jean Painlevé said and it is the title of the Criterion Collection box set of his films.

p. 188 – 'The key here … ' is from Jean Painlevé's *Traitement éxperimental d'une hémorragie chez le chien* (1930).

p. 192 – 'Once … ' is paraphrased from Jean Painlevé's *Les amours de la pieuvré* (1967).

p. 192 – 'A father … ' is based on a story Jean Painlevé tells in *Jean Painlevé Through his Films* (1988).

p. 203 – 'He picked up … ' is very loosely paraphrased from a description of molluscs in Jean Painlevé's *Acera* (1972).

p. 203 – 'The miles … ' is based on *Les Champs magnétiques* (1919) by André Breton and Phillippe Soupault.

p. 210 – 'A wind … ' is paraphrased from Guillaume Apollinaire's 'Train militaire' (written in 1915, published posthumously in *Poèmes à Lou* (1947)).

p. 223 – 'Stuff this … ' refers to *Un chien andalou* (1929) by Luis Buñuel and Salvador Dali.

Fights Cited

Pernell Whitaker vs. Oscar De La Hoya

Pernell Whitaker vs. Diosbelys Hurtado

Vince Phillips vs. Kostya Tszu

Paulie Malignaggi vs. Vyacheslav Senchenko

Paulie Malignaggi vs. Juan Diaz I

Roberto Duran vs. Davey Moore

Jersey Joe Walcott vs. Rocky Marciano

James Toney vs. Vassily Jirov

Aaron Pryor vs. Alexis Arguello I

Zahir Raheem vs. Erik Morales

James Kirkland vs. Glen Tapia

Acknowledgements

I am very lucky to have been supported in my life and creative work by too many lovely friends to name, and I hope that if they read this they'll know I'm talking about them right now.

I am proud and delighted to publish with Coach House Books, a press that publishes art and makes books artfully, and am eternally indebted to Alana Wilcox, who is the reason Pillow exists in the first place and persists until now.

I gratefully acknowledge the support of the Ontario Arts Council and the Canada Council for the Arts.

I'd like to thank Ellen Zweibel and Peter Showler, whose home (and homemade sauna) I squatted in as I wrote this book, James Leo Cahill for introducing me to the Surrealists (Zoological and otherwise), Jeremy Hanson-Finger for dragging nets with me, Eden Fine Day and Les George for showing me what stories are, Ariel Caldwell for helping me turn a page, and Pasha Malla for helping me write a first book in the first place.

Thanks to my family, to whom I owe all and love very much.

And thanks to Zani and Djuna, who make my life a joy to live.

Andrew Battershill is the husband of the writer Suzannah Showler and the father of Djuna. He is the author of two previous novels. His work has been longlisted for the Giller Prize, shortlisted for the Kobo Emerging Writer Prize, and he was the winner of the 2019 ReLit Award in the novel category. He works as a public librarian on the unceded homelands of the xʷməθkʷəy̓əm (Musqueam), Sḵwx̱wú7mesh (Squamish), and səlilwətaɬ (Tsleil-Waututh) Nations.

Typeset in Albertina and Six Hands Brush.

Printed at the Coach House on bpNichol Lane in Toronto, Ontario, on Zephyr Antique Laid paper, which was manufactured, acid-free, in Saint-Jérôme, Quebec, from second-growth forests. This book was printed with vegetable-based ink on a 1973 Heidelberg KORD offset litho press. Its pages were folded on a Baumfolder, gathered by hand, bound on a Sulby Auto-Minabinda, and trimmed on a Polar single-knife cutter.

Coach House is located in Toronto, which is on the traditional territory of many nations, including the Mississaugas of the Credit, the Anishnabeg, the Chippewa, the Haudenosaunee, and the Wendat peoples, and is now home to many diverse First Nations, Inuit, and Métis peoples. We acknowledge that Toronto is covered by Treaty 13 with the Mississaugas of the Credit. We are grateful to live and work on this land.

Edited by Alana Wilcox
Cover design by Ingrid Paulson
Interior design by Crystal Sikma
Author photo by Suzannah Showler

Coach House Books
80 bpNichol Lane
Toronto ON M5S 3J4
Canada

mail@chbooks.com
www.chbooks.com